COMANCHE COUNTRY

Joe Kelly has bought a half share in Travis Neal's ranch in an area reputed to be Comanche territory. While searching for his missing partner, Kelly encounters a Comanche war party, three former Confederate soldiers fleeing a killing in Mexico, the Mayne family and a renegade gang. The arrival of a self-promoting US marshal adds to their problems. Kelly and the Maynes must face hostile Indians, white murderers and a fanatical lawman before they can reclaim their respective ranches, and then another problem arises. Suddenly there is the danger that friends will fall out, and more lead will fly before the situation is resolved.

R10   RD023245   J

OD

LARGE PRINT

Central Support Unit
Catherine Street Dumfries DG1 1JB
tel: 01387 253820 fax: 01387 260294
e-mail: libs&i@dumgal.gov.uk

Dumfries and Galloway LIBRARIES Information and Archives

UK

CUSTOMER SERVICE EXCELLENCE

24 HOUR LOAN RENEWAL ON OUR WEBSITE - WWW.DUMGAL.GOV.UK/LIA

COMANCHE COUNTRY

COMANCHE COUNTRY

by

Greg Mitchell

Dales Large Print Books
Long Preston, North Yorkshire,
BD23 4ND, England.

British Library Cataloguing in Publication Data.

Mitchell, Greg
    Comanche country.

    A catalogue record of this book is
    available from the British Library

    ISBN   978-1-84262-757-0 pbk

First published in Great Britain in 2009 by
Robert Hale Limited

Cover illustration © Gordon Crabb by arrangement with
Alison Eldred

The right of Greg Mitchell to be identified as the author of this
work has been asserted by him in accordance with the
Copyright, Designs and Patents Act, 1988

Published in Large Print 2010 by arrangement with
Robert Hale Limited

Dales Large Print is an imprint of Library Magna Books Ltd.

Printed and bound in Great Britain by
T.J. (International) Ltd., Cornwall, PL28 8RW

ONE

The feeling was there again, an apprehension that kept him looking about and expecting trouble despite seeing nothing amiss. Joe Kelly, you are frightening yourself, he thought. Even if the Rutledge boys claimed they saw a Comanche a few days ago, the raiders would almost certainly have moved on. War parties were fast-moving, hitting hard and fleeing quickly. Two years after the Civil War had ended, government troops were moving into Texas and with them came the prospect of strong and swift reprisal. Consequently the marauders dared not linger in the land that had once been theirs.

The Rutledge ranch with its heavily shuttered windows and rifles protruding from loopholes, had resembled a small fortress when he rode up to it and the family had expressed surprise that he had reached them unmolested. Theirs was the last ranch between civilization and the ranch that Travis Neal had hoped to reclaim in what people called Comanche country.

Clem Rutledge had told him bluntly, 'You're crazy to be going any further. You're getting deeper into Comanche country if you do. My boys saw a Comanche not far from here the other day. I told your partner, Travis Neal, that when he came through here. But he wouldn't listen – was all too keen to see that run-down ranch that his folks left him while he was at the war. You were crazy to buy in with him. We ain't seen a sign of him since he rode out there to take a look. I warned him not to go. And there's other folks who have gone out into that Buffalo Creek and Wolf Mountains country that we ain't seen neither. I reckon them Comanches got them all. Stay here with us; we can always use an extra man.'

Kelly had refused the offer explaining that

his partner might need his help even more if he was in trouble. He felt that he had to go, but to be on the safe side he left his pack mule at Rutledge's. It would only be an encumbrance if he had to ride for his life and he could always collect it later if all was well.

He was as well prepared as a single rider could be. He was young, fit and mounted on a good bay gelding that had both speed and staying power. On each hip he carried a Whitney .36 revolver and a new Ball, .50 calibre, repeating carbine rode in a loop on his saddle horn. He would he able to give a good account of himself – provided he was not taken completely by surprise. And with Comanches such a possibility had to be considered.

The country around him was rolling grassy hills with small stands of oak and cedar showing on the crests. In the distance to his right, the Wolf Mountains rose in a mass of dark-green pines amid stony ridges against the clear blue sky. His path lay to the south of the mountains through shallow open valleys where the light green foliage of willows and cottonwoods showed against the long, yellow grass. Such places looked cool and inviting, but he avoided these and stuck to more open ground. They were too tempting to travellers and ideal spots for ambushes.

His worries increased when, far ahead, he sighted buzzards circling in the sky. The sign was an ominous one, but it did not necessarily mean that Neal was dead. It could be a dead animal, he told himself. If there had been a fight, horses might have been shot, but his partner had been well armed and could still be holding out. The thought of abandoning him to his fate was not even considered. He had to investigate.

He had not known Neal for long; they had met by chance in a saloon. Kelly had sold a few mustangs he had trapped and broken and Neal was on his way home from the war. He was down on his luck but was keen to rebuild the ranch that had fallen into ruin during his absence. Lacking the money for essential supplies, he had offered Kelly a half share in his ranch for a hundred dollars and his assistance to get it back to being a working concern. It had been abandoned since his parents' death halfway through the war and would take a considerable effort to become viable again, but the opportunity had looked a good one to Kelly. It had offered him a new and more settled life and, as he saw it, a once-in-a-lifetime opportunity. It would be a gamble. Hard work and a certain amount of luck would be involved. Now he was beginning to have doubts about his luck.

Neal had made no secret of the fact that the Comanches had raided in the area but was confident that they posed no serious threat now that men were returning from the war. However, the sight of circling buzzards brought back grim memories and Kelly began to wonder if his partner had fatally underestimated the Indian problem.

A faint breeze was blowing, swirling

among the low hills and changing paths to the extent that Kelly could not really gauge its main direction. But the breeze was bringing a scent that had his horse snorting and nervously looking about. The rider felt the hair rising on the back of his neck. The feeling was worse because he saw no reason for it. He fought the urge to wheel the horse about and gallop back to Rutledge's ranch. Just think a while, he told himself. For all he knew, the Comanches could be following him and he would run into them. By keeping to the middle of the fairly wide, shallow valley, Kelly had a clear view of the immediate area around him but was still within rifle shot of the hills on either side.

Suddenly his horse swung its head, ears pointed toward the hilltop on his right. Kelly's gaze followed his mount's and his previously imagined fears became reality. A mounted Indian was there sitting statue-like on a grey pony. A long-barrelled gun was cradled in his arms. Even as Kelly watched, another warrior joined him, the pair remaining still and menacing on the crest.

Where there were two there were bound to be more and the warriors need not have shown themselves if they had not meant their presence to be menacing. But why would they risk a fight in the open?

Kelly rode on and noted that the two Comanches fell a little to the rear but stayed with him. He was contemplating turning away from them at right angles when a couple more riders appeared on the other side of the valley. They too moved parallel to him but positioned themselves to cut him off if he was to turn back from his original course. His safest course seemed to be straight ahead. The country was fairly level and open and he knew that his horse had plenty of pace. But the escape route was too obvious.

'They're herding us,' he said, partly to himself and partly to the horse. 'As long as we keep heading the way we are, they won't come too close. Somewhere ahead there's an ambush.'

There was no easy way out of the trap. One of the warriors on the left had a lance and both appeared to be armed with bows and arrows. Even shooting from horseback the Comanches were unlikely to miss with their arrows. The two on the right looked slightly less dangerous. Both had firearms, but one held what looked like an old smooth-bore musket and the other had most likely a single-shot weapon of some kind. Two years after the end of the Civil War, repeating rifles were still not common among the nomadic tribesmen. Kelly's chances looked better against the warriors armed with guns. Without drawing his carbine he was able to work the trigger guard and lever a cartridge into the chamber. The weapon was designed to hold twelve shots, but could also take military ammunition and he had loaded it with seven more powerful and more readily available Spencer cartridges. The reduced cartridge capacity did not worry him because he had the feeling that the issue would he resolved one way or another before the magazine was emptied.

Aware that every forward step his mount took was probably bringing him closer to danger, Kelly decided that he would try to break from the trap while he still could. He suddenly spun his horse to the right and spurred it up the hill. As he had expected, a cry went up from the Indians and the warriors on the ridge rode to intercept him. He eased his bay slightly because it suited his plan for the warriors to cut him off. Seconds later they were in his path but he had the advantage. They had to twist sideways and fire downhill, not a situation that leads to accurate shooting.

The foremost warrior fired a hasty shot from his long musket sending a jet of grey powdersmoke down the hill. But his shot went wide. Aware that he could not reload quickly, Kelly saved his first shot for the other rider who was bringing his carbine to bear.

Both men fired at once but, as often

happened when men fired from different levels, the warrior shot high and missed. The white man had the easier shot and spilled his opponent from his pony's back. Kelly was levering another cartridge into his carbine as he charged at the brave on the grey pony.

The Indian dropped his useless rifle and rolled down on the off side of his horse supporting himself by one heel hooked across its spine and an elbow in a horsehair loop around the animal's neck. His face reappeared over his mount's back followed by the muzzle of a Colt Dragoon .44.

But Kelly wasted no time on small targets, firing into the horse behind the shoulder. At the least it would shatter the animal's heart, but the bullet, at that range, also had a chance of going through into the Comanche. The stricken horse jumped high in the air as the warrior sought frantically to get clear of the arm loop. He had not succeeded though when his mount crashed on its side and trapped him underneath.

The man was out of the fight, so Kelly did not wait around to see how badly he was hurt. He could hear the other braves crossing the valley and wanted to stay well out of bow range. The chance existed that the Indians might not pursue as they often tempered their vengeance according to the losses that the war party had suffered. Older warriors sometimes decided that one scalp was not worth heavy losses that could not be replaced. But young bucks took a much more reckless approach.

The reverse slope of the hill was steep but the bay horse went down it in a series of stiff-legged bucks and hurdled the dry watercourse at the bottom. Then Kelly touched it with the spurs to gain a bit more ground where it was more level underfoot. Here he could take full advantage of his horse's speed. With open ground ahead, he could risk a look behind and when he did, he saw that the two riders were still following. He had expected that they would because it was well known that Indians would always chase those who ran from them.

If the race was to be a long one, the extra weight carried by his horse would start taking its toll so he eased back the bay lest it should exhaust itself too soon. But he did not intend running for much longer. With his repeating rifle he had a big advantage and looked about for a suitable place to turn the tables. A short distance ahead, he saw a clump of cottonwood trees and there, using them for cover, he resolved to end his flight.

He was almost at the trees when, to his horror, he saw that horses were concealed there but he was too close now to turn away. Frantically, he slammed his carbine back into its loop and drew a revolver in the faint hope that he could shoot his way out of the trap.

Even as Kelly sought his first target, rifles boomed and gunsmoke rolled out of the thicket.

TWO

Kelly was amazed that the unseen shooters had missed him but then, as he burst in among the trees, he saw that he was among white men. Had they shot at him and missed, or were they shooting at his pursuers? He sat his horse back on its haunches and looked around, ready to shoot if necessary.

'Be careful with that gun,' a voice called urgently, 'we're on your side.' The speaker was a tall man in a Mexican sombrero who held a smoking Sharps carbine in his hands. He was about forty with a craggy face and a short, sandy heard. A pair of big Remington .44s rode butt forward in open holsters on his hips.

Kelly checked the bay and holstered his revolver. 'I'm sure glad to see you.'

'You're about the only sonofabitch that is,' growled another man, as he stepped from behind a tree. This one was slightly younger with a dark complexion and at first glance could have been taken for a Mexican but his southern drawl indicated that he came from somewhere north of the Rio Grande. He too, wore a pair of large revolvers and a bowie knife in a sheath hung from his gunbelt. 'We missed them Comanches,' he growled as he pointed with his carbine. 'They're gettin' away.'

'Let them go, Happy,' the tall man ordered. 'There's not much chance of hitting them at this range.' Then he turned to Kelly. 'You should be more careful where you go for a morning ride.' A big hand came out. 'I'm Tad Carstairs and that smiling *hombre* there is Happy Jacobs.'

'I'm Joe Kelly. You were sure in the right place at the right time.'

'That does make a change.' A young, solidly built man led three horses forward. 'I'm Harvey Machin and I'm pleased to know that someone is glad to see us. Of late, our positioning and timing has been somewhat astray.' He was not as heavily armed as his companions, wearing just one gun of a type unfamiliar to Kelly.

Briefly they discussed the Comanches before carefully approaching the issue of what each was doing in such dangerous territory. It was never polite to ask too much about another man's business, but normal observations revealed much. One glance at the narrow-chested Mexican ponies and dinner-plate horns on the saddles confirmed that the trio had come out of Mexico recently.

'I hear things were pretty lively for a while across the Rio Grande,' Kelly said cautiously.

'Too lively for us,' Carstairs admitted. 'It seemed like a good idea at first until everything went to hell in a hand basket. We heard that Maximilian, that Austrian duke, was keen to recruit former Confederates for his war with the Juaristas. A lot of us ex-rebs went down there to fight for him, but we picked the losing side. We seem to be getting pretty good at that.'

'It sounded hetter than surrendering,' Machin said. 'We got a bit of irregular cavalry work for the Austrian duke and the French, but things got too serious. Neither side was taking prisoners and then the French troops decided they had had enough and went home. They were the backbone of old Max's army and after that we had no chance. We saw the error of our ways just in time.'

'That was round about the time the Juaristas shot poor old Max,' Carstairs added. 'We reckoned that a trip north of the Rio Grande would be real good for our health, so here we are. What's been happening while we've been away?'

Kelly thought for a while. 'Things are not too good. Federal troops are leaning mighty heavily on us folks in Texas, and the Comanches and Kiowas have been raising hell. Half the ranches have been abandoned.

Nobody in Washington cares what happens here and troops that should be chasing war parties are stretched mighty thin.'

'What about the Texas Rangers?' Machin asked.

'They were disbanded because of the part they played in the war. Heaven only knows if they'll ever be re-formed.'

The trio looked disappointed.

Carstairs gave a rueful smile. 'We were sort of hoping to join them. We don't have a lot of qualifications for more peaceful pursuits.' He asked Kelly, 'What do you do for a living?'

'My partner, Travis Neal, and I have a cattle ranch west of here over on Buffalo Creek. We didn't know that the Comanches were on the prod around there. Travis went on ahead a couple of days ago; I was held up waiting on supplies. You fellers haven't seen a white man on a big grey horse over the last couple of days, have you?'

The trio looked from one to another as if each was reluctant to break bad news.

Finally Machin said, 'We found a grey horse dead a few miles south-west of here. It had been shot and it looked like there had been a fight. We saw no sign of a rider though.'

'Chances are the Comanches took him off somewhere to torture him to death in their own time,' Happy added. 'They like doin' that.'

Kelly was forced to admit that the man was probably right. Indians would not attempt to conceal or carry away a dead body. His future plans were now in even more doubt than they had been. Though anxious to find out his partner's fate, it would be too risky to continue with his original plan. It seemed safest to join the others until they were out of the danger area. When he enquired about where the others were headed none seemed to have any preferences.

'I guess the closest town will do us,' Carstairs said. 'Can you direct us there?'

Kelly pointed to the north. 'If we head that way for a couple of miles we should pick up a trail. It leads east back to a town called Bondsville. I'll be going that way for a while, although I will have to take a detour to the Rutledge ranch on the way to pick up my pack mule.'

'That sounds good to me,' Carstairs told him. He turned to his companions. 'Who's for seeing the sights of Bondsville?'

For the fifth time since leaving camp at sunrise, Dan Mayne stopped the six-mule team, stood on the wagon box and looked around. His lined face wore a frown as he looked at the map held by his wife, Ethel. The map was hand-drawn and crude with no proper scale. He pushed back his hat and wiped a sleeve across his perspiring forehead. 'Danged map,' he complained. 'We should be able to see a line of hills on our right by now, but the only ones I see are on the left.'

'Perhaps we are facing the wrong way,' his wife of twenty-five years suggested calmly.

'If we are someone has turned the sun

around too. We're lost, Ethel – well and truly lost.'

Mayne was so absorbed with their problems that he scarcely noticed his daughter Anna as she halted her paint pony beside the wagon. Despite days on the trail, she still looked a picture even with the crumpled black sombrero jammed on her brown curls and dust on her divided skirt and boots. The smile on her face always lifted her father's spirits. She was their youngest, aged nineteen.

Norton, the eldest, was twenty-three, a large capable young man, who drove their second wagon. He was always dependable and lately his father had started to value his opinions.

Their other child, Ollie, two years younger than his brother, was riding nearby, loose-herding half-a-dozen spare horses.

'Looks like Daniel Boone is lost again,' Anna joked to her mother.

Her father was fast losing his sense of humour but forced a smile. He might have reacted differently if one of his sons had made a similar remark, but it was hard to become angry with Anna. 'This map that the land agent drew us is worse than useless. He said that Buffalo Creek would be easy to find, but it flows south. From the position of those hills all the water here would flow north.'

'Could we be on the wrong side of those hills?' Anna asked.

Her father's frown deepened. 'I think we are, but getting the wagons over them might not be easy and I'm not sure how far we would have to travel to get around the western end of them.'

Norton brought his wagon alongside and halted the team. 'I reckon we're lost, Pa,' he called across to Dan.

'You're right. This map that Hannan gave us doesn't line up with anything around here. Those hills can't be the ones on the map. There's no mistaking the direction that water runs and all the water courses are running in the wrong direction.'

'There's no point in wearing out our teams,' Norton suggested. 'Let's find a good campsite and I'll get on a horse and ride up to see what's on the other side of those hills.'

'I could go,' Anna suggested.

'You could, but you ain't,' her older brother corrected. 'There's Comanches and Mexican outlaws and all sorts roaming this country. It ain't safe for you.'

'Mister Hannan said that it was a safe place,' the girl argued.

'Hannan also drew this map,' her father said. 'We know how accurate that was. The word around Bondsville was that the Comanches still raid through here every so often. It's unlikely they would be here now that the country is opening up but it's best to be careful.' He turned again to Norton. 'When you go, take a rifle with you as well as your six-shooter and keep your eyes open.'

'I always do,' the elder son assured him.

It was an hour later when the family found a suitable place to halt. There was a small trickle of water and a patch of open grassland suitable for grazing their stock. They parked the wagons in the shade of a few cottonwoods.

Leaving Anna to ride herd on the horses and mules as they fed, Dan and Ollie unharnessed the animals and set about constructing a rope corral using the wagon wheels and some trees as anchor points. They fully expected that they would make no further progress that day and all agreed that the stock would be safer corralled at night.

Ethel collected some water for the camp and paused a while where Dan was securing a rope to a tree. 'You're expecting trouble, aren't you? Do you think it's safe to send Norton into those hills alone?'

'I'm just being careful. Chances are things are safe enough but he's younger and more alert. If trouble starts his chances of getting back here are a lot better than mine would be. You know I wouldn't send him out if I knew there were Indians out there.'

'The trouble is,' his wife reminded him, 'that nobody really knows where Indians are or are not.'

Norton had saddled the powerful black horse he always rode and took a Spencer rifle from the wagon. Opening the butt trap he fed in seven cartridges and closed the magazine. As an afterthought he reached into the cartridge box, took a handful of bullets and transferred them to a pocket in his vest. Then he led the horse over to where his parents stood. 'I could be gone a couple of hours. I'll ride to the top and see what's on the other side and if I can see something like Buffalo Creek is supposed to be, I'll try to find a way for the wagons to get over. It might be dark before I get back so tell anyone who's on guard to challenge before they shoot.'

'We'll build up the fire,' his mother said, 'so you can see where we are.'

'That might not be a good idea, Ma. I'll find you if I'm late.'

THREE

Kelly led the way up the steep slope, leaning forward in the saddle and holding his horse's mane to assist it as much as possible. Behind him, the others, riding in single file, did the same. The scrambling hoofs raised dust and sent loose rocks rolling back down the hill.

'We're leaving a good trail if those Indians decide to come after us,' he told Carstairs when they reached the summit. 'I don't like stopping on the skyline like this but we'd better rest these horses soon. Your ponies are just about done in. That was a hard climb.'

'You seriously don't reckon those few Comanches would risk taking us on again so soon after us chasing them off?'

Kelly swung down from his saddle and patted his horse's sweaty neck. 'The trouble

31

is that we don't know how many are really in that war party. A big bunch will often break up into a few smaller ones, but they can come together again mighty quick. A few flashes with a mirror, a smoke signal or even a pre-arranged meeting can combine those little scattered groups in a very short time.'

Happy stepped down from his weary pony. 'The way our luck's been runnin' lately there's probably a hundred of them red devils on our tracks and they've sent for the Kiowas as well just to make sure we don't get away.'

Machin had dismounted and was searching through a saddle-bag. Finally he found what he sought and displayed a handful of copper cartridges. 'I hope you're wrong, Happy,' he said. 'Apart from six in my gun I only have seven more rounds for my fancy French shooting iron.'

Kelly was curious. He had seen by the butt protruding from the holster that Machin's gun was different. 'What sort is it?'

The former confederate drew the gun and

displayed it. 'It's a French gun, fires them European pin-fire cartridges. The hammer hits a little pin at the base of the cartridge and sets it off. They're much quicker to load than conventional cap-and-ball revolvers. Trouble is that the spare ammunition went with the French and I haven't been able to get any more. We had to leave Mexico in a hurry.' He might have said more but a frown from Carstairs who was standing behind Kelly, caused him to finish abruptly.

Though he pretended not to notice, Kelly suspected what had happened and had the distinct feeling that he was not in the best of company. How far could he trust them? But he did not have time to ponder his problem.

'Nobody move,' Happy whispered urgently. 'Just turn your heads slightly and look what's comin' along the top of the range.'

Their eyes followed his and they sighted a long procession of Comanche warriors emerging from a clump of dark-green pines. Though still half a mile away they could see flashes of colour from blankets, a rippling line of various coloured horses and the glint of sunlight on steel.

'Do you think they saw us?' Kelly asked.

'I don't think so because we are half screened by the brush – but they'll see us soon.'

Carstairs studied the scene for a while and said quietly, 'In a couple of minutes they'll be behind another clump of trees. While they can't see along the crest we'll start down into the trees on the other side. They might not see us down there among the pines.'

'They'll cut our tracks in a minute or two,' Kelly said. 'But I reckon you're right. There's nowhere here that we could hold out against that many. We might have a better chance down in the trees.'

Machin was watching the approaching riders. 'They're nearly all behind the trees. Get ready to go ... no, just a few more. Now, let's go.'

They mounted quickly and set their mounts down the slope hoping to be concealed among the trees before the procession came into view again. The pine needles partially muffled the sounds of their horses but occasionally a rider went too close to a tree and noisily snapped off a small branch. There was no way they could move in silence and even if the braves were still out of earshot, their horses would he picking up the sounds. Their tracks would be plainly visible when the Indians reached them and all knew that their discovery would only be a matter of time.

Kelly was well mounted but his companions, ponies had seen too many long rides and short rations and did not have much galloping left in them. The white men could not keep ahead of the pursuit for long. Their best chance lay in finding a good spot to stand and fight.

They were on the lower slopes when a shout went up from the Comanches. Their tracks had been discovered.

Kelly was leading the way when he heard a horse crashing through the trees on his left. His heart gave a bound. Were they cut off already?

Then a young white man on a large black horse burst out of the foliage. 'Don't shoot,' he called as he approached. His face was pale and he appeared badly shaken as he ranged his horse alongside Kelly's. 'I saw you on the hilltop and was thinking of joining you when I saw the Indians. My folks are camped not far from here. We have to warn them.'

'Where are they?'

'They're about a mile to the east at the foot of these hills. They have a couple of wagons.'

'How many men?'

'Two, but my mother and sister can shoot as well.'

'Lead on. We might have some chance if we all keep together.'

Kelly eased back his horse until Machin caught up. 'There's white folks not far away. Follow the *hombre* on the black horse.'

He was drawing his carbine when Carstairs and Happy drew level.

'What are you going to do?' the big man demanded.

'I'll try to slow them a bit. There are some white folks ahead and the shots will warn them of trouble.'

'There's too many of them Injuns,' Happy shouted. 'You can't stop them.'

'I know that, but if I just slow them down a bit, your horses might just get you to a safer place.'

Carstairs wasted neither time nor breath but showed his appreciation with a brief salute as he galloped past.

Kelly halted at a spot where he could command a view of a broad clearing, He did not dismount but waited with his carbine ready to greet the first warriors to come into view. He could hear the horses crashing through the brush and the excited yells of the warriors as they approached. Suddenly they were in sight, painted for war and as eager as hounds on the scent. A shout went up when they saw the white man on the other side of the clearing.

Kelly fired and heard the solid thump as a bullet hit the leading horse. He reloaded quickly and sent the next bullet at the second rider who was checking his mount to avoid colliding with the stricken horse in front. He moved his mount slightly and fired another shot into the horsemen whose numbers were increasing rapidly. The wounded horse finally went down and Kelly fired again into the riders trying to get around it. The pursuers, thinking that they had ridden into an ambush, reined in their ponies. But there were seasoned warriors among them and the white man could see them turning their mounts at right angles to work around both of his flanks. He thought he had knocked another rider from his mount when the firing pin clicked on an empty chamber. It was time to go.

While all was confusion, he turned his mount and galloped away. The Comanches did not follow immediately, because repeating rifles were still not common on the frontier and they were not certain as to how many men were opposing them. Kelly had gained a hundred yards' start before the pursuit began again. When he finally emerged from the trees, he saw that his companions were travelling in a straggling line behind the rider on the black horse. He was close enough to see their legs and arms working frantically as they urged the last bit of speed out of their failing horses.

Seconds later, a high-pitched war cry behind him announced that the Comanches now had all their enemies in view.

In the distance Kelly could see a rider on a paint horse herding loose stock into some sort of makeshift corral between the wagons. The stranger on the black horse was shouting something to the people at the camp, but the distance was too great to understand what he was saying. A rifle fired from the camp. The range was too long for accurate shooting but it served notice on the scalp-hunters that they could expect casualties if they pushed their attack.

The man on the black horse was first to the wagons and he dismounted there. After putting his horse through the gate, he stood beside it with his rifle ready to give covering fire for the others. One by one the three men from Mexico urged their weary mounts into the corral and dismounted. The animals stood there, heads down, exhausted and streaming with white sweat. Kelly saw puffs of gunsmoke as the new arrivals opened fire on their pursuers. He glanced over his shoulder and, to his relief, saw that the Comanches had halted at long rifle range. Easing the bay back to a steadier pace, he steered it into the corral and the young man pulled a rope across the entrance and fastened it. Dismounting quickly, he drew his carbine, tied the reins around his mount's neck and turned it loose with the others.

Someone in the camp fired a couple of shots, but Carstairs bellowed, 'Stop shooting. It's a waste of lead. You'll need every bullet when they get closer later.'

FOUR

Kelly filled his carbine's magazine as he dodged among loose stock to find a place that gave him a good view of the attackers. There was little time for introductions, but Dan hurried from one new arrival to another and made himself known. He paused briefly at a wagon to get Machin a war-surplus, rifled musket and a handful of paper cartridges and caps. The latter was quickly ramming home a load when Mayne reached Kelly.

'I'm Dan,' he said, as he thrust out his hand. 'You came in with my son, Norton. That young feller over there by the other wagon is my younger son, Ollie. My wife Ethel and daughter Anna are in the wagons.'

Kelly shook his hand. 'I'm Joe Kelly. Under better circumstances I'd be pleased to meet you, but for a family man I figure you're in a bad spot here.'

'Don't I know it. Do you know much about Indians?'

'I've had plenty of fights with them. They raided our ranch regularly as I was growing up. But I'm still learning about them. They're not easy to figure out. How about yourself?'

'This is the first time I've ever seen hostile Indians. I saw plenty of fighting in the war, but this is different. What do you reckon they'll do?'

Kelly looked across the plain to the group of riders milling impatiently around. 'If they reckon they have the numbers, they might try to charge right over us but most likely they'll test our fire power first. No Indian tribe can afford to lose braves these days so they try to avoid costly attacks. I think they'll make little probing attacks to see where our weaknesses are before they try a final charge at us.'

Machin was fiddling with the rear sight of

his borrowed rifle. 'How far out do you reckon they are?' he called to Happy.

'Too far; six hundred yards at least. Don't waste a shot on them.'

Machin patted the old rifle affectionately. 'I carried one of these for three years during the war and I know I can land a slug in the middle of our feathered friends out there. The way they are bunched it's sure to hit a man or a horse.'

'Won't make any difference in the long run,' Happy predicted gloomily.

'Go ahead,' Carstairs encouraged. 'If you happen to hit a man, it won't help their confidence, because they know they will lose others on the way across that plain.'

Machin knelt and rested his left forearm across a wagon tongue as he sighted carefully and thumbed back the big side hammer. The rifle roared and seventy grains of black powder charge kicked savagely against the shooter's shoulder The onlookers had ample time to see the result as it took more than a second for the big .58

calibre bullet to reach its mark. The compact mass of men and horses suddenly erupted into frantic movement.

'You hit something,' Carstairs shouted. 'They're scattering out of range.'

'They'll be back,' Happy reminded.

He was right. While the main force moved back, a widely spaced group of riders whooped and came rushing across the plain brandishing weapons, their ponies' necks stretched as though seeking to be first in some sort of race. Future tactics would depend upon the strength of opposition encountered.

'They're just testing us,' Kelly said. 'Let's hold our fire and see how close they're prepared to come in. They can't shoot accurately like that with guns but be careful if they get into arrow range.'

The riders rapidly came closer, twenty of them at most, still maintaining their wide spacing. The shot that missed one would not strike another. None changed course as though they intended their first charge to take them right through the whites' defences.

'They're close enough,' Kelly yelled. 'Let 'em have it.'

A ragged volley rang out from the camp apparently without scoring a hit.

Dan, Norton and Kelly all had repeaters and now they fired rapidly while the others reloaded. An unexpected rattle of shots from behind the driver's seat of a wagon caught Kelly's attention and he looked to see a young girl, her face a mask of concentration, pouring out a steady stream of lead from a Henry rifle.

The Indians veered off, dropping over their ponies' sides as they did so. A shot pony somersaulted, but its rider was picked up by another warrior in a fraction of a second as the Comanches sought to flee back to longer range, all except one warrior. Obviously wounded, he clung to his horse's mane and drove it straight at the gap between the wagons, determined to die among his enemies.

Machin's shot knocked the man from his mount as it jumped over a wagon tongue. Drawing his revolver he rushed to finish off the Comanche but found he was already dead. Pausing only to snatch the dead warrior's breech-loading carbine, he tore the buckskin pouch of cartridges from his belt and returned to the firing line.

But the Indians had learned what they wanted to know. This time they advanced in a wide crescent formation with the wings outspread to encircle the camp while keeping at long range. The front and right sides of the defences faced on to open country but their left side was anchored in a belt of trees and attackers could use these for cover.

'They'll be hard to shift once they get into those trees,' Carstairs observed.

All defenders agreed that the trees were their weak spot but they did not have the numbers to hold the attackers out of them.

'We can stop them coming across the open ground,' Machin said. 'But those in the trees are going to be one hell of a problem, 'specially if they advance on foot.'

'I have a repeater,' Kelly said. 'I'd best cover that side.'

'I'll help you.' He had forgotten about the girl in the wagon. Anna displayed her Henry rifle. The sixteen shots in the Henry would not hit as hard as the .50 calibre slugs from his carbine but the weapon's high rate of fire was a great asset.

Carstairs snapped a shot at some riders out on the plain. 'Best get under cover and keep your eyes open,' he called. 'They should be among the trees by now. If things get too bad on that side call out and Norton can come across with his repeater too.'

The Comanches were among the trees. Dismounted now, they were running from one tree to another as they approached the camp. Their approach now was less spectacular but much more dangerous.

Kelly fired a couple of shots at the closest warriors and sent them back under cover, but knew that the respite was only temporary. He heard Anna fire from the wagon too and hoped that she had extra protection inside as the sideboards would not stop bullets. An arrow thudded viciously into the wagon barely a foot from where Anna's rifle showed but the archer disappeared behind a tree again before the others could shoot back. In ones and twos the warriors were advancing, screeching as they ran in erratic patterns to confuse shooters, loosing their arrows and shooting their guns but always working closer More than one missile thumped solidly against the trunk or tore strips of bark off the tree that sheltered Kelly.

Thirty yards away a painted warrior suddenly broke cover and charged forward. Anna's shot picked him off and he collapsed, but the rush had started. A squat Comanche, his face hideous with red, yellow and black war paint, discarded his empty gun and bounded straight at Kelly with an upraised tomahawk. A slug from the carbine hurled him back but another two were darting forward between the grey

48

trunks of the cottonwoods.

Anna's rifle was no longer heard and he had no way of knowing the reason. Had she been hit, or had she run out of ammunition? There was no time to satisfy his curiosity and Kelly dared not take his eyes from the charging warriors. Then, with a sound that froze his heart, the rifle clicked empty. Reloading was out of the question.

Putting the carbine aside, he drew one of his revolvers. He had twelve shots and then both Whitneys would be empty too. 'Over here!' he called in the hope that Norton or the others might have noticed his situation. He could hear someone still firing but nobody came to his aid because they too were heavily engaged.

His attackers were developing some respect for his shooting but showed no signs of retreating. Arrows and bullets had narrowly missed him and Kelly knew that his assailants would not continue to miss for long. There was time for two more shots and then a whistle pierced the din of battle. He had heard such whistles before. They were made from the leg bones of eagles and were often used to signal an Indian charge.

Kelly drew his second revolver. This is it, the finish, he told himself.

FIVE

Anna's rifle sounded again and, as Kelly peered through the gunsmoke from his revolvers, he saw that the Comanches were running back through the trees. More than a little puzzled by what was happening, he wasted no further shots but loaded more cartridges into his carbine while he could.

Shouts of triumph were coming from the other defenders too.

'They're running,' Ollie shouted. 'We've beaten them.'

Kelly was feeling too relieved to argue, but knew that the Comanches were far from being beaten.

'It's soldiers,' Ethel called. 'Thank God.'

The defenders turned to see a distant group of blue-coated cavalry approaching in skirmishing order with drawn carbines.

'I never thought I'd be happy to see those blue coats,' Carstairs said, as he studied the oncoming riders.

'I wouldn't go celebratin' too soon,' Happy growled. The look that he gave his companions indicated that there could be good reasons for his lack of enthusiasm.

The patrol halted briefly at the camp. The young officer leading them was plainly eager to pursue the distant tribesmen but paused long enough to introduce himself as Lieutenant Wyler. 'Anyone hurt?' he asked, as he reined in a horse that seemed as impatient as its rider.

'Reckon not,' Mayne admitted.

'How many hostiles?'

'Maybe forty or fifty.' Mayne guessed there were about thirty soldiers. 'They might he carrying a few casualties, but you will need to be careful.'

'There are more troops on the way. Captain Gillespie is not far behind me. Tell him I'm after the war party. It's not often we catch them in the act.' The lieutenant wheeled his horse as he spoke. 'I might see you later.'

'That's if you live long enough,' Happy growled, as the soldiers rode away in a clatter of equipment and sabre scabbards.

Kelly turned to Anna. 'I'm mighty glad to see you in one piece, miss. When your shooting stopped I thought you might have been hit.'

The girl laughed nervously. 'My rifle didn't throw out an empty shell properly and I had to clear it before I could start again.' She held out a small hand. 'I'm Anna Mayne.'

Kelly shook her hand gently. 'I'm Joe Kelly, pleased to meet you. I sure didn't expect to see a family out here.'

'Were on our way to our new ranch. Pa bought it recently.'

'Seems like the whole country is starting

to open up,' Kelly told her. 'I bought a half-share in one south-west of here on Buffalo Creek. But I think that the Comanches got my partner.'

'I'm sorry to hear that, but our place is on Buffalo Creek too so we will probably be neighbours. What about your friends here?'

'I only met them this morning but they've proved themselves handy men to have around. Seems they're just back from Mexico where they found themselves on the losing side of the war they have been fighting down there.'

The trio in question were in earnest conversation with Dan and Ethel Mayne when the others joined them.

'Surely you don't need to go before you have a meal,' Ethel was protesting.

'Unfortunately we do,' Carstairs said quietly. 'But we would greatly appreciate it if you could spare us a bit of grub to take with us.'

'That's the least we can do,' Dan assured him. 'When would you want it?'

Machin was nervously watching the direction from which the soldiers had come. 'Right now would be much appreciated.'

Ethel turned to her daughter. 'Give me a hand, young lady. These men are in a hurry.'

When the women were out of earshot, Mayne asked, 'Are you boys in any trouble?'

'We're not sure,' Carstairs admitted. 'We never surrendered after the war and went to Mexico instead. The Yankee army might not feel too friendly toward us. It's best if we don't meet them. I'd much appreciate it if you forgot who we were and don't recall where we were going. Given the condition of our ponies every hour we gain could be mighty important.'

Norton was checking the state of the livestock in case some had been wounded by stray shots. He found a mule with a bullet hole through its ear and a pony with a graze across its rump. He brought both across to a wagon and tied them there for his father to dress the injuries. Ollie, much to his mother's disgust, had been collecting weapons from the dead Indians. He had a butcher knife in a beaded sheath and a much-abused Navy Colt and some ammunition for it. There was a worn trade musket, but after a glance at it the boy decided that its value was only as a souvenir and threw in into a wagon. A wiry Indian pony was nervously sheltering among the Maynes' stock. Its late rider had jumped it into the camp. 'Mr. Machin,' Ollie called, 'there's an Indian pony here. You shot its owner. Do you want it?'

Machin strolled across to where he could see the animal. He shook his head. 'You keep him. My Mexican mustang is a better type. I'll stick with him.'

Anna asked Kelly, 'Will you be going with the others, Joe?'

'No. I still have to find out what happened to my partner. He might still be out in the brush somewhere. He has no horse and might be hiding from the Comanches. He could even be wounded.'

'But what about the Indians?'

'They'll be high tailing it out of this country. With at least two army patrols in the area, they won't stay around.'

'That's a relief because it looks like we will be stuck here for the night. Pa says a bullet has weakened one of the wagon tongues and he will have to repair it by wiring on a sort of timber splint. There's only green wood available here so he needs to harden it in hot ashes overnight. Why don't you stay here tonight? An extra gun will be very welcome.'

Carstairs and the others were ready to go. They shook hands with the Maynes and Kelly and exchanged wishes of good luck. Then Carstairs told them, 'It might be an idea if you folks all turned your backs so if you are questioned later, you can honestly swear that you didn't see where we went.'

'Suits me,' Kelly said. 'But are you sure that people will be after you after so long away?'

'There's always a chance they might,' Machin said, after choosing his words carefully. His wary choice of words implied that the trio had seriously transgressed someone's laws.

Happy was less circumspect. 'You can bet your boots someone will be after us.' He turned to his companions. 'Time we was long gone from here.'

The former rebels had been gone for an hour when the next cavalry patrol arrived. Their leader was a small, grey-haired captain and a buckskin-clad scout rode beside him. But there was a civilian there too, bigger than the cavalrymen, with a stern expression, dark eyebrows and a dark, drooping moustache. Behind the three men rode about thirty troopers, their blue coats liberally sprinkled with red dust.

The patrol halted at the camp and dismounted in the shade. Mayne and Kelly walked across to the newcomers. The captain, Gillespie, introduced himself, Ed Milroy, his scout and Henry Glynn, a United States marshal.

The latter glared about him as though

expecting trouble. Glynn suspected everyone and had been a member of the United States Marshals Service since the 1850s where he had shown great zeal in tracking down runaway slaves under the Fugitive Slave Act. But such activities were no longer applauded and now the situation was more complicated because he was working with people of his own colour. As an answer to the changing times, Glynn decided that it was safest to trust nobody and tell people as little as possible. He saw information as power.

Both Mayne and Kelly were a little puzzled by his presence, but knew he would eventually state his business if it involved them.

Gillespie listened intently to the account of the Comanche attack and Milroy nodded occasionally in agreement with various comments. He said he had heard many such stories and in other cases those involved did not live to relate their experiences.

Finally the captain asked, 'Did you really hold off forty or fifty Comanches with two women and only four men?'

'We had another three men here,' Mayne told him, 'strangers that the Comanches chased into the camp.'

Glynn was suddenly interested. 'Where are they?'

'I have no idea. They rode on after the Comanches bolted. They didn't say where they were going and out here it's not polite to ask.'

'Did they give any names?

Mayne thought a while. 'One said his name was Carstairs. There was a younger one called Machin and one called Happy.'

For the first time a note of excitement crept into the marshal's voice. 'It's them. I knew they'd be coming through here somewhere.' He turned to the captain. 'We have to get after them.'

'I'm afraid not, Marshal. My first priority is to catch up with Lieutenant Wyler. He's probably outnumbered and the Comanches are likely to turn on him. It's not often we get this close to a war party and I do not intend diverting this command. You can go after your men on your own, or you can stay with us until we get near a telegraph station and call for more help, but my men are soldiers not lawmen. We'll water the horses here and make sure every man has a full canteen and then we're moving on.'

'But those men are killers,' Glynn protested.

Gillespie looked hard at him. 'So are the Comanches. They've killed a lot more.'

'But they have not killed an officer specially appointed by the President – and in a foreign country too.'

SIX

The marshal was still protesting when he rode away with the patrol a short while later. He had questioned the civilians and had taken many notes, but there was little that they could tell him. For his part Glynn was not willing to disclose any details of the crime that the former rebels had committed. 'That's not for you to know,' he had snapped, when Kelly asked about the alleged murder. 'It's government business.'

'I don't like that man,' Ethel said of the marshal.

'I doubt if even his mother likes him,' Dan suggested. 'But he has a job to do. Carstairs and the others didn't seem too bad to me though. They could have held us up and taken supplies and even fresh horses, but they didn't. I'd sure like to hear their side of the story.'

'What are you going to do now?' Kelly asked.

'First I have to fix that wagon tongue so we'll be here for at least a day or so. Then we need to find a way over those mountains to get back on to Buffalo Creek.'

'I've been over those hills and you won't get a wagon across them. When you passed Rutledge's ranch you should have gone on to the left side of the hills. You might be able to go further west and get around them, or you might have to go back nearly to Rutledge's place and go south of the hills.'

Mayne growled in disgust and fished a well-worn paper map from his coat pocket. 'The fellow named Hannan who sold the ranch to me drew this map back in Bondsville. He should know how to get there.' He handed the map to Kelly.

It took only a quick glance to see that the hand-drawn map was wrong. 'I haven't been there, but my partner had a ranch on Buffalo Creek before the war and he went out ahead of me. I was following his tracks when the Comanches chased me over the hills. I can tell you for sure, Dan, this map is only good for getting you lost.'

'So we have to go back nearly to Rutledge's and go around the other side?'

'Most likely. I'll be going back there myself soon to pick up my pack mule. If I catch up with you later, we can go to Buffalo Creek together.'

Mayne looked at him sharply. 'You're not coming with us?'

'I still have to find Travis. I want to have a look around where his dead horse was found. Then I'll come back to Rutledge's for my mule and supplies.'

'You're crazy, Joe. There could still be Comanches running around out there.'

'I doubt it. I think they'll be heading for the Staked Plains with the army on their heels. They won't be back this way for a while.'

'When will you leave?'

'First thing in the morning. I'll give you a hand now to bury those two dead Indians and take a turn at guard duty tonight just in case I guessed wrong and the odd dismounted straggler might be about looking to steal a horse.'

Dan could only find cottonwood to repair the weakened tongue and it was green and soft. While that made it easy to square the wood he knew that he would have to season it overnight in a bed of hot ashes before it could be wired to the damaged pole. 'We might be stuck here longer than we thought if this repair don't work. Norton here, thinks that cottonwood won't be strong enough,' he told the others.

'That's right,' said the older son. 'We need hardwood.'

'If it holds together till you get to Buffalo Creek,' Kelly said, 'there are supposed to be wild cattle everywhere. You could shoot one and bind the weak spot with rawhide. That will dry on and shrink as hard as iron. You won't need to worry after that.'

'I'm glad that we'll be neighbours,' Anna said to Kelly. 'Our ranches must be side by side.'

'That's good,' he replied. 'Travis and I thought that we would he stuck out there on our own. He said they had no neighbours when he left for the war.'

Kelly was much more pleased than he could show at the thought of Anna living nearby. He was not sure if the attraction was mutual, but he was enjoying every second of her company. Her manner was so gentle and caring and it seemed strange that only a couple of hours before she had been shooting to kill with the calm deliberation of a veteran soldier. Soft and feminine she might be, but Anna was not the sort to have fainting fits. In a crisis she had shown herself to be as reliable as any man. Yes, sir, he was going to enjoy living near the Maynes.

By daybreak Kelly was starting the climb over the mountains. He wanted as much daylight as possible because he did not expect that it would be easy to discover Neal's fate. Two hours later he was descending the southern slopes of the range. To the west he saw buzzards still circling in the sky and turned the bay's head toward them. Due to their efforts and those of other scavengers, he knew there would not be much of the dead horse left but it would be a good starting point.

The carcass was easy to find. By chance he approached it from downwind and he could smell it long before he actually saw it. A few buzzards reluctantly took wing at the rider's approach to join the others already circling as though waiting their turn.

There were hoofprints and boot prints around the dead horse, but Kelly had expected that because the three former rebels had told him that they had found the carcass. Three Spencer shells, already tarnishing in the weather, lay close together on the churned-up ground. Neal, like many former soldiers, liked Spencer repeaters and had owned one. It appeared that he had fired at least three shots while sheltering behind his dead horse.

The saddle-bags had been removed from the saddle and ransacked and this too Kelly had expected but discarded nearby he found a few items that puzzled him. He saw a .44 calibre bullet mould, a common enough item in any frontiersman's baggage, but something eagerly sought by Indians. There was a box of matches that had been later trodden underfoot and not far away lay a small, circular orange tin that normally contained percussion caps. Kelly kicked it idly with the toe of his boot and, to his surprise, it rattled. When he picked it up and opened it, he found that the container still had a few caps in it. The three particular items apparently were ignored by the attackers and Kelly frowned. Something was wrong. To a Comanche, a bullet mould, a few matches and some percussion caps, represented great value but they were commonplace items to white men. Still half expecting to find an answer to the puzzle, Kelly studied the ground. The hoofprints had the clear impressions and sharp edges of those left by shod horses. It was possible that some Comanches could be riding shod horses stolen from white men, but nothing could explain the desirable items that the Indians seemed to have ignored. It was looking increasingly like Neal had been attacked by white men. But where had he gone?

Assuming that Neal had escaped from the area, Kelly circled it about fifty yards from the dead horse, he found nothing except the prints of shod horses coming and going. He tried again. The next circle found some bullet-marked trees and nearby, another Spencer shell. He guessed that his partner had been engaged in a fighting retreat through the trees. His hopes rising, Kelly began searching in the direction indicated. But as rapidly as his hopes had risen, they fell again. On a rock and a nearby patch of bare ground, he found what he was sure was dried blood.

Not far away he spied a thin trickle of water falling from a rocky shelf above. Reason told him that a wounded man might head for the water so he dismounted, hitched his horse to a tree and started pushing his way through the undergrowth.

It was the buzzing of flies that told him where he needed to go. Just at the edge of the stream, Travis Neal lay dead, his face pallid, open eyes staring at the sky and his clothing stiff with mud and dried blood.

Though he had been half expecting such a sight, Kelly stopped in his tracks. He had been hoping that Neal had somehow eluded his ambushers and that he would find him alive. It appeared that he had escaped the ambush but died later from his wounds. The buzzards had not found him because he had been alive probably until the previous day and had been hidden in the thick brush. A Spencer rifle lay nearby and Neal's Remington .44s were still belted around his waist.

Kelly's next task was far from pleasant but it had to be done. He unbuckled the gunbelt and began searching the dead man's pockets. The search yielded a silver watch, smashed by a bullet, a few dollars in change, a pocket knife, a pipe, tobacco and matches; nothing of any importance. He remembered that the partnership agreement and ranch deeds had been left with the lawyer in Bondsville and guessed that any personal papers Neal might have been carrying, were in his saddle-bags. He had not found any but resolved to have a further search when he went back to the dead horse. If Neal had relatives they would want to know what had happened him. Having no means to dig a grave in the rocky ground, he could only cover the body with brush and stones to keep scavengers away.

The task was almost finished when Kelly heard his horse shift nervously where it was tied in the nearby brush. The animal was standing, head high and ears pricked as though trying to see through the brush that screened it. Then he heard the voices.

SEVEN

The human voice carries a long way in areas where there are no other distracting sounds and Kelly, although he could not yet discern the actual words, knew from the tone that he was hearing white men. He also knew it was unwise to consider that all he met in that area would be friendly.

Cautiously he peered through the thin

foliage of a thin mesquite bush and saw three riders approaching the dead horse. All carried rifles ready for instant use. The foremost rider sported a thick black beard and was dressed in range clothing. He was not a big man but rode alertly on his roan horse and something about his manner gave him a dangerous almost predatory look. The man about a half horse length behind, wore fringed buckskins and had the dark features of a half-breed. He looked relaxed, almost lazy, slouched in the saddle of his pinto pony but his type, Kelly knew from experience, missed little of what was happening around them. The other rider was a big man with a short brown heard. His clothes looked like a townsman's suit that had seen plenty of dust and little cleaning. The tip of a holster showed under the coat on the left side so it could be rightly assumed that he was carrying two revolvers. His horse was a large, sorrel animal that seemed better quality than the mounts of his companions.

They were close enough now for Kelly to

hear Black Beard say, 'I don't see no buzzards except around the horse. Maybe he
ain't dead yet.'

'If he ain't, he's mighty tough,' the half-
breed said. 'I know I scored two solid hits on
him. He's probably lying up there in the
brush and the buzzards ain't found him yet.'

Brown Beard said in a hoarse voice, 'Have
you pair considered that he might still he
alive? We really need to find out before we
tell Hannan that we got him.'

Kelly had heard enough to know that he
would be in trouble and a hasty search
would soon reveal his presence.

'You won't get me going into that brush
after him,' Black Beard informed his companions. 'He might still be capable of pull-
ing a trigger. In that brush you could be on
the muzzle of his gun before you saw him.'

'I wouldn't worry,' the half-breed said
casually. 'I know he's hit bad. My shots
knocked him down twice. He has no horse
and is carrying lead. He might get away a
short distance but he'll die.'

'That's the trouble with those Henry repeaters,' Brown Beard complained. 'They don't hit hard enough. They're really only a pistol cartridge.'

'I heard tell that Yankee soldiers with Henrys were killing people at eight hundred yards' range during the war.'

Black Beard gave a derisive snort. 'Anyone killed by a Henry at that range was mighty unlucky. The front sight would completely cover a man at that distance. No shooter could see a man properly. Cherokee, old friend, don't believe everything you hear.'

The half-breed changed the subject. 'So what do we tell Hannan about Neal, Russ?'

The brown-bearded man replied, 'We tell him that he is dead and we left him out in the brush for the buzzards. If that ain't quite the truth now, it soon will be.'

Kelly relaxed slightly when it became apparent that the three riders would not venture into the brush, but he was far from at ease with what he had discovered. The killers had deliberately targeted Travis, the one with the brown heard was named Russ, the half-breed was Cherokee and they appeared to be working for someone named Hannan. The name sounded familiar but he could not recall meeting any Hannans recently.

The three riders halted briefly and Black Beard shouted, 'Can you hear us, Neal? I hope you're dyin' real slow. Give our regards to the coyotes and buzzards.'

Kelly fought back the urge to raise his partner's carbine and blast the bearded one out of his saddle. I'll get you, he vowed silently. You have not seen me but I know what you three coyotes look like.

Allowing the riders to get out of the area, Kelly slung Neal's holstered revolvers from his saddle horn, picked up the Spencer carbine and fully loaded it. As his rifle also used the Spencer round, ammunition was no trouble. Then he cautiously emerged from cover. The riders' tracks led in a north-westerly direction keeping in the trees that grew on the slopes of the mountain range.

He had to he careful because Indians always watched their back trail and some cautious white men followed the same practice. It was nerve-racking following tracks and trying to ensure that he did not ride into an ambush at the same time.

Then his luck changed. He saw the three tiny figures ride across a distant clearing and knew that the killers were taking no precautions. He picked up the pace then and closed the gap between them. Gradually the hills on the northern side became lower and it became obvious that the mountain range was running out. He guessed that a short ride around the western end of the range would take him into the Buffalo Creek country. Travis had told him that the creek rose on the south side of the range and flowed in a southerly direction. But one thing was certain: the country was too rough for wagons and the Mayne family would need to retrace their steps and go around the eastern end of the hills.

Emerging from the trees on the hillside,

Kelly saw a wide expanse of grassy flat dotted with feeding horses. At first he thought they were mustangs but then noted that most were too big and that no foals could be seen. Quickly he turned his mount back into the timber. If those horses were grazing in the open someone would be watching them. Dismounting, he hitched the bay to a tree and crept to the edge of his cover. He was in time to see the three horses he had been following, unsaddled and rolling in the dust before joining those feeding. Then he saw the men and the camp.

They were resting in the shade talking to a fourth man who stood nearby holding the bridle of a saddled horse, obviously the herder watching over the loose animals.

Back among the trees Kelly could see a canvas tent fly slung over a rope and boxes and bundles stacked beneath it. A few poles running from tree to tree indicated the presence of a temporary coral, probably for holding the stock at night. He could not help wondering how the Comanche raiders had not found the place but then remembered the half-breed. Had they reached some sort of agreement with the Comanches?

He had seen enough for the time being but as he crept back to his horse, Kelly silently vowed to return. There would be a day of reckoning.

Carstairs looked at his pony and his frown deepened. The animal was reluctant to move and stood with one foreleg extended. This was no time for a horse to get a stone bruise. His companions' mounts were showing their ribs and did not have many more rides left in them, but at least they could still walk. 'Looks like I'm back in the infantry,' the tall man said.

'Danged horse picked a fine time to go lame,' Happy complained.

Machin looked at the crippled pony. 'The way he's pointing that leg, it's not something that will get right in a day or two. Now we're really in trouble. Where are we going to get another horse out here?'

'We need three new horses,' Happy muttered. 'The other two won't last long either and we need more grub.'

Carstairs thought a while and finally said, 'Those Mayne people had some spare horses. Maybe we can do some sort of deal with them.'

Machin disagreed. 'You're loco, Tad. We have no money and who in their right mind would swap three healthy horses for two that are worn out and one that could be lame for months. And we need food as well.'

'We have to get out of this border country,' Happy argued. 'The law's certain to be looking for us. Uncle Sam is sure to feel a bit peeved about us shooting that spy of his.'

'Rodgers was a lowdown skunk,' Machin said angrily. 'He sold us out to the Juaristas. There was no need for him to do that.'

'It was a gesture on behalf of the Yankee government,' Carstairs explained. 'What better way to impress Juarez and his men about being on the same side? It's not as if us former rebels are of any value to them.

By now they'll know that we got away and I reckon they'll he watching for us to show up. We need to get a long way from here, but at present we don't have the means to do it. I think we might have to take what we need from the Maynes.'

Machin objected strongly. 'They're decent folks, Tad, and they were good to us. We can't rob them. What do we do if they decide they don't want to get robbed? Have you thought of that?'

Carstairs snapped back angrily, 'Do you think I haven't? Damnit, Harvey, if you know a better way out of this fix, tell us. You don't have to stay with me. You and Happy still have horses.'

'We ain't splittin' up now,' Happy announced, 'not after all this time. I don't like takin' anything from the Maynes, but maybe we can make it up to them somehow later.'

'I don't know how.' Machin was not convinced. 'Up till now we have never got on the wrong side of the law. We even killed Rodgers in self-defence, although a Yankee court might think different. Those folks will reckon we're a pack of low-down coyotes.'

'But at least we will be living, low-down coyotes,' Carstairs reminded.

'For how long?' Happy asked.

EIGHT

Henry Glynn's narrow face bore an impatient frown as he listened to the Morse code coming through the electric telegraph and saw the operator scribbling on his message pad. He dared not disturb the freckle-faced young operator because he was working on what might have been the most important message in the marshal's career, but the suspense was hard to take.

Finally the clacking noise ceased. The young man tapped an acknowledgment, tore off the message and handed it to Glynn. It had been claimed that if the marshal ever smiled, it would break his face but his features remained intact when he allowed the corners of his mouth to turn upwards. There it was: authority to raise his own posse of five men and permission to charge the cost of wages and supplies to the federal government. Finally he had a case that would win him a big reputation. The President himself would surely be taking an active interest in this one. Glynn's ambition soared. The exercise with the cavalry had been a waste of time except that it had made him a little more familiar with the area of border country where he was sure that the former rebels had crossed the Rio Grande. He would raise his posse as quickly as he could and would begin searching the area between Bondsville and Buffalo Creek where the men had been sighted. Because it was considered Comanche country, few people lived there so it would be good for hiding. But even fugitives had to eat and by all reports, the wanted men were travelling with few of life's necessities. They would need the help of others to survive and because the area was so sparsely populated, he knew that he could find the information he sought by questioning relatively few people. Now Henry Glynn would really make his presence felt.

Kelly caught up with the Maynes not far from where they had rounded the eastern end of the hills and swung west again to head for Buffalo Creek. He had made a diversion to Rutledge's to pick up his pack mule and to inform them about what had occurred. Three generations of the Rutledge clan lived at the ranch and their white-bearded patriarch, Clem, had amassed a wealth of information about the surrounding countryside. He had expressed no surprise when Kelly told him of discovering a group of white men living at the far end of what the Rutledges had called the Wolf Mountains.

'I know there's someone out there. My men see their tracks occasionally when they are going to or from Bondsville. They give this ranch a wide berth but we see their tracks,' the old man said.

When asked about the presence of hostile Indians, Clem had laughed. 'Sonny, the Mexican Comancheros ain't the only ones who trade with the Comanches. Some of us Anglos do too. But they leave me alone and I leave them alone. I know there's a few folks who have headed out that way and never came back. But I warned them if they came through here, just like I warned you and your partner – for all the good it does.'

The wagon tracks were easy to follow and Kelly caught up with the Maynes sooner than he had expected. The repair on the wagon tongue was working loose again. Dan had set up camp by a small stream and the evening meal was cooking when Kelly arrived.

'You're just in time, Joe,' Ethel greeted. 'We have fresh beef tonight. Let your animals go and get ready to eat.'

Dan was busy with an awl and twine

stitching a wrapping of wet rawhide on to the wagon tongue. He had replaced the unsatisfactory cottonwood repair with the barrel of the trade musket Ollie had picked up after the fight. It was less bulky but much stronger. Anna and Norton were nearby briskly rubbing large chunks of raw beef in a tub of coarse salt. Other pieces were draining on a wide board in the shade.

'Norton shot a wild cow,' Anna explained. 'Pa needed some hide for the wagon tongue so we thought we would save as much meat as we could.' She shook her hands. 'I hate this salting. Any little cuts or scratches on your hands really sting.'

Norton laughed. 'I thought your neck would be hurting more than your hands, Sis. Do you know, Joe, that she has been looking behind us all day? It was almost as if she was looking for someone.'

Anna blushed. 'One day I'll murder you, Norton.' She added rather lamely, 'We all need to look around out here in Comanche country. Don't take any notice of him, Joe.'

Though secretly pleased, Kelly said nothing.

That evening, around the camp-fire, they discussed future plans. There were many wild cattle in the area and all agreed that their ranches would be almost fully stocked.

'We won't die of starvation,' Dan said, 'but we'll need to find a market for some stock just to keep money coming in. After we bought the ranch and six months' supplies we're not exactly cashed up.'

Kelly knew exactly what he meant. His own meagre savings were almost gone because he had bought his half share of the ranch and most of the supplies. Neal had returned from the war almost broke. 'We might be able to collect a few mustangs,' he suggested. 'But it's hard work and folks won't pay much for them. I saw a few mustang signs west of here the other day before the Comanches chased me over the mountain.'

'Anna's glad they did,' Ollie teased.

Her cheeks flushed with embarrassment

the girl turned and glared at her brother. 'One day, Ollie–' But she left the rest unsaid.

'Don't kill him until after he stands his night watch tonight,' Norton laughed.

'I'm glad to hear that you are still keeping watches,' Kelly told them. 'I found a camp of white men at the western end of those mountains. My partner's dead and I know that it wasn't Comanches who did it. Rutledge knows there are white men out here but doesn't know who they are. Their camp is not a long way from Buffalo Creek and there will be trouble with them.'

Dan looked hard at him. 'You seem mighty sure.'

'I am sure, because I'm going to cause it. I intend making life hard for those murdering sonsof–' Just in time Kelly remembered the presence of the ladies. 'Comanches or not, nobody at our ranches will be safe until those men are shot out or driven out. But there are three of them that I don't intend to let ride away.'

'How many are there?' Ethel asked nervously.

'At least four, and Rutledge suspects that they are coming and going from Bondsville so there are probably more. Some might live in town. According to Rutledge, a few folks have headed out into this country recently but none ever came back again. The Comanches got the blame but they only survive by keeping moving. They can't afford to stay too long in any one area. These white men are behind the disappearances for sure.'

Norton looked worried and scanned the heavily timbered country around the camp. 'If you're right, they could be getting ready to hit us right now.'

'It's possible, but I think they'll let us get closer to Buffalo Creek. They didn't look to be in any hurry when I saw them. They probably know that you were on the north side of the Wolf Mountains and are waiting for you to almost walk into their camp. When they see your tracks going back, they might think you have gone back to

Bondsville, but eventually they'll see smoke from your camp-fire or one of their scouts will see us on the move. We might have a couple of days but they will find us.'

Dan rose from his seat on a log and pushed back his hat. 'I'm not sure it's a good idea to go on just now. We won't break camp tomorrow. It will give that rawhide on the wagon tongue time to shrink hard and more importantly, it will give us time to think things over. I have a feeling we might have rushed into this deal a little too quickly.'

Norton was horrified. 'We can't turn back now, Pa.' He asked Kelly, 'Are you turning back, Joe?

'No, I'm not, but I don't have a family to look after and I'm not hampered by wagons. I can hide my camps but two wagons can't be hidden for long. Your pa's talking good sense.'

Ollie came up with another suggestion. 'What if Norton and I stay with you, Joe, and Ma and Pa and Anna take the wagons back to Bondsville? Once we get rid of those bushwhackers, we can send for the others.'

'This family stays together,' Ethel announced firmly. 'Whatever we do, we all do it together.'

Anna sounded annoyed too. 'I don't intend to be sent out of the way. I did my share of fighting Indians the other day. Isn't that right, Joe?'

'You sure did,' Kelly was forced to admit. 'But this will be a different sort of fighting. These men will be better armed than the Comanches were.'

'That doesn't make them bullet-proof,' Anna said stubbornly.

'And you ain't, either,' her father reminded.

Further argument ceased abruptly when one of the horses in the night corral neighed. It was answered almost immediately by another horse on the dark slopes of the mountains.

'We have company,' Kelly whispered, 'and we can't count on it being friendly. Best put out the campfire.'

NINE

They waited, clutching rifles and peering into the gloom. The heavy tread of horses, breaking of twigs and dislodged rocks rolling down the slope made a stealthy approach impossible.

'Who's there?' Dan challenged. Already his rifle was at his shoulder.

'It's us, Carstairs, Machin and Jacobs. Don't shoot.'

'Come in real slow and don't try anything rash until we have a good look at you.'

Three men emerged from the trees, two mounted and one leading a limping horse.

Carstairs said in an aggrieved tone, 'Why so touchy, Dan?'

'Maybe it's because I know now that you three are wanted for murder. What are you doing here?'

'We're in trouble,' Carstairs admitted, 'and we need help.'

'We could get into a heap of trouble helping you. There was a marshal with that second military patrol. He said you murdered a US Government official down in Mexico.'

'So that's the story they're telling. We did kill an American after he deliberately led us into a Juarista trap. He got a few of our friends killed and we were very lucky to get out alive. It seems that your government decided to sacrifice a few of us Rebs to show Juarez that they were well and truly on his side.'

'Why are you back here?'

'Because our horses are nearly finished and we are starving.' Carstairs thought it wiser not to mention what their original plan had been. The noisy horse had ruined all plans for a stealthy approach.

'We could get into had trouble helping you.' Mayne was weakening and a note of uncertainty had crept into his voice.

Ethel joined the conversation then. 'Come in, boys,' she called. 'Ollie get the fire started again. We have visitors to feed.'

One by one, the others emerged from their defensive positions. Norton lit a lantern and Ollie soon had a fire blazing again. Eagerly the hungry men listened to the clatter of dishes while Ethel and Anna prepared a meal for them.

Kelly was particularly interested in what the three rebels had seen but they had been mostly in concealment in case of army patrols. They knew nothing of the men camped at the other end of the Wolf Mountains. Eventually the subject of replacement horses came up, but Mayne made it clear that he had no intention of swapping three fit horses for two worn-out ones and a lame animal. 'I can help you with grub but I can't afford to lose any horses. We'll need them all when we start work at Buffalo Creek,' he said.

Then suddenly Kelly had an idea. 'I know where we can get a few horses for you fellers and you'll be doing us a big favour at the same time. Are you interested?'

'We sure are,' Happy announced. 'But there's some sort of catch, ain't there?'

Henry Glynn looked back with pride on the small cavalcade that he was leading, five well-equipped, newly appointed, special deputies and a pack animal. He had been very selective in the men he had chosen, picking only those who would follow him unquestioningly with little regard for the rights and wrongs of the situation. He would do all the thinking that needed to be done.

Telegraphed enquiries to lawmen around the area where the rebels were last seen made him confident that they had not been to any of the surrounding towns. It seemed they were hiding out in the Wolf Mountains otherwise someone would have spotted them. Glynn was sure, too, that someone had to be aiding them. There was a limit to the time that men could survive just on wild game. The most obvious suspects were the

Mayne family. He was sure that they knew more about the three men than they were admitting. Glynn trusted only one member of the human race – himself. He lived in a world where black was black and white was white and there were no shades of grey. At times he had broken the law to procure convictions but excused this on the grounds that such measures were necessary to bring guilty parties to justice. Once he had decided that a person was guilty, he selectively ignored any facts that might have proved otherwise.

He had chosen Evan Passlow as his lieutenant, a large, unimaginative ox of a man whose loyalty had easily been bought with the promise of future fame. Passlow would do whatever Glynn ordered without question. It was easy to motivate his uncritical posse. They were avengers, he told them, specially selected to avenge the murder of Gabriel Rodgers, a great American patriot, killed while protecting the American way of life from the corrupt powers of Old Europe.

The name 'Rodgers Avengers' had a nice ring to it, but he decided against the title. People might forget his part in history if he put too much emphasis on the dead agent. As he rode Glynn speculated mainly upon how best he could insert himself into history.

'So you reckon this Mayne family know more about those rebels than they said?' Passlow asked, as he moved his mount closer to his leader's.

'Of course they do. People enjoy keeping information from those who are in the best position to use it. Chances are they're being bribed to keep those outlaws supplied. When we catch up with them, I'll soon get the truth out of them.'

'Do you reckon they'll give us any trouble, Marshal?'

'They'll try, Mr Passlow, but it won't do them a lot of good. I'll show them who's top dog around here. We have a hand-picked team and anyone who crosses us will come off second best. This is not a game. At the first sign of trouble we will shoot first and ask questions later. I won't exactly cry if none of this crowd makes it to court. We don't want some fast-talking lawyer to get them off the hook later.'

'How long before we catch up with this bunch, Marshal?'

'It might take us another couple of days but they have wagons and will be travelling slowly. They're in pretty rough country.'

'We'll soon make it rougher for them,' Passlow said enthusiastically. He was going to enjoy being famous.

Cherokee took a swig from the jug of white lightning and passed it to Sam Preston who was stretched out in the shade on a saddle blanket. 'When do you reckon we should hit those wagons that Hannan sent out?'

Preston took a swig, grimaced, waited till he got back his breath and replied. 'Best give them another couple of days. The closer they are to Buffalo Creek, the easier it will be to move stuff later. If anyone should get away, like that Neal *hombre,* we don't want them close enough to reach Rutledge's.'

Russ Tilden, also reclining in the shade, reached for the jug. 'Give me a swig before you finish the booze.'

'I reckon this stuff could finish us before we finish it,' Preston said, as he surrendered the liquor. 'Hannan won't he expecting quick results so we should be able to take our time with this job.'

'Not like the last job,' Cherokee laughed. 'I'll never forget the look on his face when he heard that Neal *hombre* had showed up to claim his ranch. Hannan was certain he'd been killed in the war. Wasn't there some sort of partnership deal involved with that ranch as well?'

'Damned if I know,' Tilden mumbled. 'I ain't up on all the legal comings and goings of land deals. I'm doing quite well without busting my guts on a few acres of bad land somewhere or rounding up cattle that nobody seems to want. Do you know that a fat steer's only worth about seven dollars here in Texas?'

Cherokee helped himself to another jolt of white lightning. 'Last time I was in town I heard that some ranchers are trailing their cattle to Missouri and Kansas. Heard they was getting thirty dollars a head for them there. The cattle game could be pickin' up. There's a lot runnin' wild out on Buffalo Creek.'

Tilden snorted. 'There's also hell's own trouble rounding them up and I couldn't think of anything worse than trying to hold a bunch of crazy longhorns on a bed ground at night. The slightest thing sets them critters running. There's better money just shooting people.'

'There will be till someone shoots the wrong person,' Cherokee mumbled. 'Sooner or later that's gonna happen.'

'You worry enough to be a white man,' Tilden muttered. 'Hannan has things sewn up pretty well. He knows who it's safe to shoot and we can always blame the

Comanches if folks get suspicious.'

'Maybe I am just all ignorant half-savage, but have all of you smart white men figured who to blame when the Comanches finally get chased out of here? Last time I was talking to Red Hands, he reckoned it was getting too dangerous to come into this country now.'

'You should leave the thinking to us,' Tilden teased. 'You half-Injuns don't have the equipment for it. It could be months before anyone finds out what happened to the Mayne family and after that length of time ain't no one can say that it wasn't Comanches that did it.' He sat up and looked about. The horse herd was grazing on the flat and another man was sitting by his saddled horse guarding them. 'Roy's keeping a good eye on the horses, so I reckon I'll just shut my eyes for a while.'

'You'd best save your energy,' Preston mumbled sleepily. 'We have a bit of serious killing ahead soon. Don't strain your trigger finger in the handle of that jug.'

TEN

'I think I can solve your horse problem,' Kelly told the three rebels as the latter hungrily attacked the meal that Ethel had prepared for them.

Happy looked at him suspiciously. 'What will it cost us?'

Kelly looked around to ensure that the Mayne family were out of earshot before saying, 'Just a few hours of your time is all I want but we'll need Dan's help too.'

Carstairs paused between mouthfuls. 'Let's hear what you have in mind.'

Kelly pointed to the north-west. 'Just over these hills there's a camp where a bunch of killers are hiding out. I know they killed my partner and I think they probably killed other folks as well. I also suspect that they'll soon be coming after us.'

'So you want us to help you take care of 'em?' Machin said.

'Not really, unless it becomes necessary. I want you to help me steal their horses and you can take your pick of any you want.'

Carstairs sounded puzzled. 'But what about those killers?'

'I just want them stranded out here on foot because I intend to pick them off one by one. I want them to know they are being hunted and I want them to know how their victims must have felt.'

'You make all this sound easy.' Happy was still suspicious.

'How well-guarded are the horses?' Carstairs was interested now.

'By day there's a mounted herder keeping an eye on them as they graze but by night I suspect that they are let go in hobbles. They're in good condition so I reckon they're getting plenty of grazing time. The feed there is the best for miles around so I don't think they would stray far when hobbled.'

'So it's just a simple case of a bit of horse-stealing?' Happy said. 'It sounds too easy. What if someone tries to stop us?'

'We shoot him, but avoid killing if possible. I prefer to do that myself later.'

'Where does Dan come into this?' Carstairs asked.

'We need to borrow three of his horses for you. That's as far as I want the Maynes involved. I don't think they would like to know my personal plans for those killers. Now, how do you like the idea?'

All agreed that they had expected something much worse and were relieved to learn that they could solve their horse problem without needing to steal from friends.

'You can count us in,' Carstairs announced. 'When do we start this job?'

'I'll see Dan about the horses and we could hit them tomorrow night. But remember, this is a horse raid, nothing else, and the less the Maynes are told about it, the easier they'll sleep.'

Clem Rutledge knew that Glynn's posse was coming, half an hour before it galloped into the yard of his ranch and halted in a cloud of dust. One of his grandsons had ridden in earlier from an observation post that he had established on a high hill. It was always manned when there was grass on the ground to feed Indian ponies. But, out of habit, the Rutledge clan remained behind their fortifications until they were satisfied that any visitors posed no threat to them.

Glynn looked at the shuttered windows and did not seem perturbed that the muzzles of several rifles were pointed at him. 'You, in the house, come out here,' he called.

Clem Rutledge's gravel voice came back. 'I'm giving the orders around here. Give me one reason why I shouldn't blast you off that horse – and that reason had better be a good one or none of you will get out of here alive.'

'Now see here–' Glynn was about to argue but he saw a rifle muzzle move in his direction. His imperious manner suddenly deserted him and something like panic took over. He croaked, 'Don't shoot – I'm a law officer.'

'Show me your badge.'

The marshal flicked open his coat to display a silver star in a circle pinned to his vest. 'See that? I'm the law.'

'Not round here you ain't. While I have a gun on you, I say what happens. What do you want?'

'I need some information. Can we talk privately?'

'You're damn lucky to be talking at all. Say your piece.'

'But this is government business,' Glynn protested. 'It's secret. Only certain people should know about it.'

'All us Rutledges are *certain* people. We're certain we are going to blow you to hell if you don't tell us why you are here. This is your last warning. Start talking.'

Glynn was skating on thin ice and he knew it. In an admission of defeat he said, 'I'm looking for three men who murdered a government agent in Mexico. I think they are still in this area. Have you seen any strangers?'

'There's a family called Mayne came through here a few days ago and a young *hombre* named Kelly was here yesterday picking up a pack mule. His partner Travis Neal came through about a week ago. But I reckon the Comanches got him. There ain't been anyone else. The Maynes took a wrong turn and went the wrong side of the Wolf Mountains, but my son saw their wagon tracks yesterday and they were finally going the right way toward Buffalo Creek.'

Glynn remembered his encounter with the Maynes and Kelly but pretended not to know them in the hope of gaining some extra scrap of information. 'What can you tell me about those people? Are they Southern sympathizers?'

'How in the hell would I know? I mind my own business and you should try doing the same.'

Exasperation crept into Glynn's voice.

'Those people are my business. I know they had contact with the men I'm after. They probably helped them too.'

'Well, it seems to me that you should be talking to them and not bothering me.'

'Can't we discuss this?'

Rutledge laughed. 'Some discussion that would be with you just firing questions and expecting us to answer them without giving a good reason why we should.'

'You can't do this. I have been specially appointed by the President. You'll do as I say.'

The voice that came back was cold and deadly serious. 'Marshal, I've seen hogs with better manners than you. You can water your horses at the trough near you and you can fill up your water canteen at the well, but you ain't setting foot inside my house without the right piece of paper. I'm aiming this rifle right between your beady little eyes, so go for your gun, or turn around and skedaddle.'

Glynn reefed his horse's head about.

'You'll hear more of this, Rutledge,' he threatened.

No reply came from the house.

Feeling somewhat deflated, the posse rode away.

One member, a small, red-haired man looked at the leader who had promised them so much. 'We represent President Johnson, you said so yourself, Marshal. We shouldn't be backing down like this.'

'It's all part of my plan,' Glynn lied. 'Trust me. I know what I'm doing. We don't go too hard too soon.'

'That's a relief,' the redhead muttered.

Inwardly Glynn was seething. He had not dreamt that one ignorant rancher had almost undermined the super-efficient image that he had so carefully cultivated.

'Now we head for Buffalo Creek,' the marshal told his men, 'and we'll see what these others have to say for themselves. Who knows the quickest way?'

A disturbed muttering came from the posse. Finally Passlow admitted, 'None of us knows the way. We're not from around here.'

'We could go back and ask Rutledge,' the redhead suggested.

'And you could get a window in your skull,' Passlow growled. 'We know the Maynes had wagons. We just pick up the wagon tracks and follow them.'

'We'd better find them soon because it's getting dark,' another posse member observed.

'The Maynes won't have walls to hide behind,' Glynn told his men. 'They'll answer our questions, or they'll feel the full force of the law.'

'We'll show 'em,' the redhead said with great enthusiasm. He was enjoying the feeling of power almost as much as their leader.

The display of enthusiasm revived Glynn's drooping spirits and he told himself that he had chosen well.

ELEVEN

Mayne was happy to loan the ex-rebels three fresh horses. As a naturally law-abiding man, the presence of three wanted men in the camp worried him. Kelly had guaranteed to bring the horses back when the new mounts were procured.

Ethel had dipped into their meagre supplies and provided the trio with enough food to last them a couple of days. Once remounted, the trio hoped to sell the two sound but weary Mexican ponies they had left. The lame one would remain with the Maynes to recover in time.

Norton and Ollie were keen to accompany the expedition but both their parents and Kelly vetoed the idea. 'You're needed here,' Kelly insisted. 'If things go wrong, it could get mighty dangerous around these parts.'

Anna was looking concerned as she watched the preparations. Finally she asked Kelly, 'Do you need to go?'

'Sure do. I know where those skunks are camped and if all goes well, will be bringing your horses back. It is important that we know what has happened. We can't expect the others to come back and tell us. They need to get out of this country as quick as they can.

'Be careful, Joe,' she said quietly. 'I would not want anything to happen to you.'

Though elated by her concern, Kelly pretended to shrug it off with a joke. 'Don't worry. The Devil always looks after his own.'

Machin was just tightening the cinch on his borrowed horse when Kelly brought his late partner's guns to him. 'It might be an idea if you take these. You'll have no trouble getting .44 pistol ammunition and Spencer repeater cartridges are easy to find. You can leave your single-shot carbine here with us.'

The former rebel was pleased to accept the weapons. The spirits of all three had lifted considerably when they were well-fed and remounted.

Kelly glanced at the sun. 'Time we were going,' he announced. 'We need to be over the mountains before darkness falls.'

Carstairs and the others thanked the Maynes profusely before climbing into their saddles.

'The best way to thank us is to stay out of trouble,' Ethel told them.

'It ain't as if we don't try,' Happy told her, 'but trouble seems to follow us around.'

With wishes of good luck to all concerned, the rebels followed Kelly as he led them away from the camp. They did not have a great distance to travel but the more light they had the easier the journey would be.

Four hours later, they were at the edge of the trees on the lower northern slopes of the Wolf Mountains. The sun had just slipped below the crest of the range and soon it would be dark.

'I'll go ahead and spy out the lie of the land,' Kelly said. 'Give me five minutes or so and follow. One person going ahead is less likely to make much noise. Just keep heading west and stay within the trees. I'll meet you a safe distance from the camp. There's no hurry. They'll bring in the horses, hobble them for the night and let them go again to graze. We want the horses to feed well away from the camp before we move in on them.'

Moving at a steady walk, it took more than two hours before Kelly saw the gleam of the camp-fire ahead. More importantly though, he heard the sound of a bell out on the plain. The horses had been turned loose to graze, just as he had hoped. They were still too close to the camp but would move away as the night went on. Now it was just a case of settling down and waiting.

In the distant camp, figures occasionally moved between him and the fire so Kelly could only speculate upon how long it would be before the killers settled down.

The others arrived and dismounted.

'We'll just sit here quietly until our friends

settle down,' Kelly whispered. 'I don't know when that will be.'

With time on their hands the rebels would have loved to smoke but they knew that was out of the question, firstly for concealment purposes and secondly because none had any tobacco.

'I hate all this waiting about,' Machin whispered.

'With the amount we've done over the last few years,' muttered Happy, 'you should be used to it.'

'I never got used to it,' Carstairs admitted.

Another hour dragged by, but then the watchers saw a hopeful sign. Someone was building up the camp-fire in the hope that it would burn all night without replenishment.

As the fire glowed brighter the watchers could just discern a horse tethered at the edge of the camp. 'We're in luck,' Kelly whispered. 'There's no guard. They've held one horse back to round up the others in the morning.'

'The horses are feedin' our way too and there's no moon,' Happy said quietly.

Half an hour later the animals, hopping awkwardly in their hobbles, had grazed close to where the men were concealed. Kelly took a rope and quietly emerged from cover. The nearest horse caught the movement and snorted suspiciously, but it was used to people and recognizing a man, it quickly resumed feeding. Talking quietly, he walked among the horses until they were used to his presence. Then he approached one of the less wary animals, stroked it for a while and slipped the rope around its neck. The rawhide hobbles were a little stiff but he managed to undo them while at the same time ensuring that the horse was shod. He led his first catch back to the men in the trees where the others fitted a halter specially brought for the occasion. The next one caught had worn, broken feet, so Kelly just removed its hobbles and left it. He caught another and quickly delivered it to those waiting. A third animal soon followed.

'There are your horses,' he told the delighted rebels. 'Lead them well away from here and saddle them up. Put halters on Mayne's horses so I can lead them back later. I'll catch you up to collect them. I'm going to take the hobbles off these others so they'll scatter to hell and gone. I want those murdering sonsabitches on foot.'

One by one he caught the remaining horses and removed their hobbles. To make their recovery more difficult, he removed the bell from the horse that wore it. Suspecting that some of the horses were probably stolen, there was a good chance that they would head back to their home ranges. It would be a long time, if ever, before the killers were all mounted again and that was exactly what Kelly wanted.

By the time he caught up with Carstairs and the others, they had saddled their new mounts. After brief farewell handshakes, they passed Kelly the halter shanks of the Mayne horses and turned their mounts' heads to the north.

Leading the three horses, Kelly crossed the Wolf Mountains again and got back to the Maynes' camp just after sunrise. 'All went well,' he told them. 'There was no trouble and Carstairs and the others have good horses.'

'What about those outlaws?' Dan asked.

'They can't trouble us till they get horses and that will be a long time. While they are stuck on foot I intend to make life a bit harder for them, too. But right now I'm dead beat. I'll just grab a bit of sleep over here in the shade while you are harnessing your teams and packing up.'

'So now we are finally on the way to our ranch?' Try as he might, Mayne could not keep the enthusiasm out of his voice.

Kelly stretched and yawned. 'It sure looks that way. With Indians, wrong trails and wanted men out of the way, life should be a lot easier.' He saw no point in telling them that he did not intend to leave any of Neal's killers alive. As he saw it, that was not the Maynes' business and he would have his revenge in his own time.

He estimated that it would take the killers a few days to get mobile again even if they could round up sufficient mounts.

Across the Wolf Mountains, Cherokee awoke with a splitting headache. Like the others, he had been drinking heavily the night before and was reluctant to face the glare of the morning sun.

Apart from a violent hangover, he immediately sensed that something was wrong. A familiar sound was missing. He could no longer hear the horse bell. Horses that are used to them become very adept at walking with hobbles so Cherokee was more annoyed than alarmed. He threw aside his blankets, sat up and swore at his aching eyeballs and the hammering inside his head.

'Do you have to make so much noise?' Preston demanded.

'Goldarned horses. They're gone.'

'You have a horse over there for occasions like this,' Tilden muttered from under his blankets, 'and its your turn to get the horses anyway, so get moving. It ain't as if you could eat breakfast if you feel half as bad as I do.'

Roy Parker, the last to awake, was not interested in horses. He only moaned, 'Why do we drink?'

Cherokee slung his saddle on to the black mare they had kept in the camp and a short while later rode away confident that he would find the horses on the next patch of good grass that he came to. But half a mile from the camp he saw something lying in the short grass. Upon riding closer he saw that it was a pair of rawhide hobbles. They were not broken and given their construction it was unlikely that they could have become unfastened. Suspicion began to grow as the half-breed looked about and saw the horse bell lying a few yards away. Its strap had been slashed with a knife.

Throwing himself into the saddle and ignoring the pain that the exertion caused, he came racing back to camp. 'We've been robbed,' he shouted. 'The horses are gone.'

TWELVE

It seemed to Kelly that he had just closed his eyes when he heard the thunder of horses' hoofs and a cloud of dust rolled over him as Glynn halted his posse just short of where he had been sleeping.

The marshal had a six-gun in his hand and bellowed, 'Nobody move!'

The Mayne family stared in amazement, seeing no need for a stealthy approach and then a sudden rush. The sight of the drawn gun evoked an angry response from Dan. 'What the hell do you think you're doing busting in here like that?'

'I'll ask the questions,' Glynn snapped. 'I'm top dog around here.'

'If you promise not to bite me, I'll stand up,' Kelly said, sarcastically. 'You can see my guns on the ground there. Where you nearly ran over me.'

'Don't get smart with me. You can stand up but don't make any sudden moves.'

'What has got into you, Marshal Glynn?' Ethel was far from impressed. 'Why are you behaving like this?'

'I'm on President Johnson's business. An important government agent has been murdered, Mrs Mayne, and I suspect you know the three men concerned.'

Dan started playing for time. 'If you are still chasing the same three as you were last time, we are not hiding them. You can search around here all you want.'

Kelly thought quickly. 'You've come to the wrong place but I think I know where your men are. There are three men camped on the other side of these mountains. I saw the camp yesterday when I was looking for stray horses.'

'Are they the men you saw before?'

'Sure are.' It did not matter if they were talking at cross purposes. As far as the lawman knew, the three rebels were the only strangers in the area. 'I can take you to their camp if you like. It's easy to find.'

Glynn was tempted but was loath to share the glory with an outsider. He wanted the rebels' destruction to be the work of only himself and his exclusive band of followers. 'If you give me clear directions, I can find the camp. My men are professionals and we don't want unauthorized people getting in the way.' Then, he added ominously, 'But if you're not telling the truth, you're in a lot of trouble, Kelly.'

'If you don't find those men it will be because of your incompetence rather than any bad directions you get from me.' Kelly pointed to the mountainside. 'Go straight over there and down the other side. Stay in the timber and head west. After a couple of miles you'll see a long, grassy flat on your right. The camp is on the western end of that flat and if you really want murderers, you'll find them there.'

Kelly saw no point in mentioning that the murderers might not be the particular gang that Glynn sought. He had put aside his personal thoughts of vengeance both to be rid of Glynn and to keep the Maynes out of trouble. He was sure that Neal's killers would not go quietly and after a serious clash with the law, they would be in no position to worry the ranchers on Buffalo Creek. A little more incitement seemed in order. 'Are you sure you can handle these characters?' he asked Glynn. 'Maybe I should go with you.'

The last observation had the desired effect. The lawman glared down at him with ill-concealed contempt. 'I have a hand-picked team; men I can rely on. I don't need you.'

'I'm mighty glad of that. I never did fancy getting shot,' Kelly said,

Glynn pointed his horse up the mountain, struck a heroic pose, and shouted, 'Forward, men.' Then, as an afterthought, he glared at Kelly. 'They'd better be there or you're in trouble.'

'I wouldn't want to cross you, Marshal.

I'm prepared to swear on a stack of Bibles that those killers are there.'

Mayne stood watching the riders charge into the mountain brush, trying to ride in formation as Glynn had ordered them but in country that did not permit it. He turned to Kelly. 'What are you smiling at?'

'It's not every day that a man can set two groups of people he don't like on a collision course with each other.'

Anna joined them. 'Marshal Glynn is one of the most bad-mannered, suspicious people I have ever seen.'

Her father chuckled. 'I've seen men like that before. Give a little authority to a man with a little brain and you get the marshal, or someone just like him. I seriously doubt that President Johnson would be very interested in what's happening here. He's having a lot of trouble with Congress at present and some say that he has shown a little too much concern for the well-being of former rebels. Marshal Glynn appears to be living in his own little world.'

'You can stop smiling, Joe,' Anna laughed. 'What if he captures these men alive and finds out they are not the ones he wanted?'

'He'll be hampered by prisoners and Carstairs and the others will get a much longer start.'

'But won't he come after you?'

'You are all my witnesses. At no time did I tell Glynn that the men in that camp are the ones he is after. He jumped to his own conclusions there. I think those hardcases will put up a fight and if the law cleans them out, it will save us from having to do the job later. I don't know if I should be admitting this, but I had intended to pick them off one by one, until Glynn came along. I suppose it's better that the law does the job.'

'I'm sure it is,' Anna said emphatically.

Cherokee was in a foul mood. He had argued for an hour in the camp trying to avoid being sent after the horses. He was no coward but was worried that he might have to deal with more than one horse-thief. His white companions had insisted that he was most suited to go because of his Indian blood, but in his life he had learned only the most basic tracking skills and knew that some white men were much better trackers than he was. Had he possessed the skills of his Indian mother, he would have seen where a few horses had moved into the timber beside the flat but instead he concentrated on those tracks that were clearly visible in the open ground.

It was fortunate for him that he was riding on the southern side of the valley where the trees shielded him from the gaze of Glynn's posse which was descending the slope not far from him. A breaking branch and a blast of language over a torn shirt were the first warnings he had that he was not alone. Then he heard the trampling of horses over rocks and a none-too-quiet voice calling for silence. A nearby thicket of young pine seedlings offered the best cover so he steered his horse into these and dismounted.

Peering through the green branches,

Cherokee saw six horsemen emerge from the trees on the slope. He also saw a badge glinting on the chest of the foremost rider. Who had betrayed them to the law?

With great relief, he saw them turn toward the camp. They had not seen him. Loyalty was not in Cherokee's make-up and he saw little value in trying to warn the others: let them take their own chances. He had never liked Tilden and the others anyway. It was time that he took a ride to Bondsville and the journey would start as soon as the newcomers were out of sight.

Glynn was pleasantly surprised. Everything was as Kelly had told him and he had no doubt that they would soon discover the camp. 'Keep in the edge of the trees,' he ordered quietly. 'No smoking or talking. These men are armed and desperate so don't take any risks trying to take them alive.' Noticing that a couple of posse members were looking rather nervous, he struck another of the heroic poses that he regularly practised. 'Remember men, the

President himself will hear of this action.' That statement was probably true and if he did, the name of Henry Glynn would be the only lawman mentioned; Glynn would see to that. 'Now, follow me,' he said. 'We are about to strike a major blow for the well-being of our country.'

Not far away, Parker, Tilden and Preston were nursing sore heads as they speculated upon the whereabouts of their horses.

'Cherokee will soon catch up with that horse-thief. That black mare he's riding is a good one and he's pretty good with a gun,' Parker said. 'He enjoys killing people so I wouldn't like the chances of that low skunk who took our horses.'

'What if there's more than one skunk?' Preston asked.

'Cherokee is a sneaky little back-shooter. He'll have a couple down before they realize that he's there.'

Tilden speculated, 'Maybe it was Comanches that took them.'

'It wasn't Comanches. Cherokee worked

out a deal with Red Hands. He might be a mean piece of work, but he's no double-crosser.'

'How come Cherokee gets on so well with the Comanches?' Preston enquired, because as a rule there was little love lost between the two tribes.

Parker chuckled 'Don't let the name fool you. He uses it because most folks see the Cherokees as good Injuns. But he's really part Comanche. I heard that his mother was Red Hands' sister. I know that there is some sort of family connection. That's why we have been able to trade for Comanche loot.'

'Listen, I can hear horses,' Tilden exclaimed. 'Sounds like Cherokee's back. They're in the trees – I can see them.' Then the look of anticipation turned to one of alarm. 'Holy hell! That ain't Cherokee, it's the law.'

THIRTEEN

Galloping horses can easily cover a hundred yards in eight seconds and from the time the posse emerged from the trees that was the only time the renegades had. Tilden alone had the chance to grab a rifle. His companions could only draw their revolvers and seek the small amount of cover available in the camp.

The first shot came from an over-enthusiastic rider at the rear of the posse and it grazed Glynn's left arm before landing far from its intended target. Almost simultaneously, the marshal snapped a poorly aimed shot at Preston, who was closest. The latter had been thinking of surrendering, but now had second thoughts and sent an ineffective bullet in reply. Tilden fired then. His slug struck Glynn's horse between the eyes and it crashed down, its rider's body cart-wheeling as it collided with Preston. As both men lay in a tangled heap on the ground, the lawman recovered his wits sufficiently to thrust his gun against the other and squeeze the trigger. The wounded man gave a bellow of pain or rage, so Glynn fired another shot that silenced him. Horses flashed past him, guns roared, and men shouted as the marshal struggled to one knee.

A horse skidding to a stop slid into Tilden sending the renegade and his rifle flying in different directions with the force of the collision. Passlow rode over to the man struggling to regain his wind and fired three shots into him at point-blank range.

Parker momentarily escaped death because the posse members were in each other's way. He managed to blast one of his attackers from his saddle before taking two solid hits that sat him on the ground. As he struggled to fire back, several more bullets struck him. The blood-lust was well and truly upon the posse and they continued firing into their late opponents long after resistance had ceased.

'Stop shooting, you damn fools. Its over,' Glynn shouted, as a bullet ricocheted off a stone and narrowly missed his head.

'We got the lot, Marshal,' the red-headed man cried triumphantly.

'But they got Bilney. He's dead as mutton.'

All the more impressive, Glynn thought to himself. It was best if the victory did not look too easy. His bullet-grazed arm was stinging slightly and he thought that a sling might be a nice touch upon his return to civilization. 'Start searching them now,' he ordered. 'We need to know who is who.'

'I thought these fellers weren't long out of Mexico,' Passlow said, as he lifted a tarpaulin and looked underneath. 'There seems to be household stuff here as well as saddles and harness.'

'Speaking of which,' the red-haired man said. 'Where's their horses? I wonder if we got the right men.'

Though he would not admit it, the marshal himself was having similar thoughts because the bodies on the ground did not tally with the descriptions he had been given. The cold hand of doubt suddenly clutched at Glynn's heart. Killing the wrong men would be bad enough, but what if he had wiped out a group of innocent settlers? They had been given no chance to surrender. The marshal had no option but to bluff his way through.

'Criminals gravitate to their own kind,' he said, with a confidence that he did not feel. 'These killers have probably joined up with another bunch who are likely out raiding ranches somewhere as I speak. These villains' horses were probably worn out so they were waiting here until the others get back with replacements for them.'

A man looked about nervously. 'What if they come back and catch us here. There could be a whole pack of them.'

'That's right.' Another looked accusingly

at Glynn. 'You said we were only after three men.'

The marshal laid on the flattery. 'If this last little scrap is any indication, you men can handle any number of renegades. Criminals are all cowards at heart.'

Passlow had his doubts but decided to side with Glynn. 'The marshal's right. We can take them on if we see them. They'll run like rats.'

Glynn would have liked to have someone attend to his arm but dared not risk one of the others finding evidence of what he was beginning to think was a dreadful mistake. 'I'll search the dead men. The rest of you take an inventory of the stuff in this camp.'

Parker roughly resembled the description of Carstairs so the marshal searched his corpse first. In an inside pocket of the man's leather vest, he found something he did not want to find, a personal letter addressed to a certain W. Parker. Hoping that the others had not noticed, he slipped the letter into the side pocket of his coat. When he was sure that no other evidence of identity remained, he listed the other contents of the dead man's pockets and moved to the next body. Tilden had been carrying no identification, but his name was written inside the sweat band of his hat. With his pocket knife, the lawman cut out the offending piece of leather and also dropped it in to his pocket. 'So much for Machin,' he said for the benefit of the others.

When removing the Remington revolver from Preston's dead hand Glynn's doubts increased. The letters TP had been carefully carved into the weapon's walnut butt. This time he made no attempt to hide the evidence but held up the weapon. 'This mangy coyote killed people with a stolen gun, but Mr Jacobs won't he killing any more.'

Preston did not resemble the description of Happy Jacobs but only Glynn knew that. Later he would slip the Remington into the stolen weapons recovered and would substitute a plain .44 in its place. When he was satisfied that his mistake had been covered up, Glynn now started the final process of removing the evidence. 'See if you can find a shovel in this camp,' he ordered the red-haired man. 'We'll bury these men.'

'Shouldn't we be taking back their bodies?' Passlow asked.

The marshal gave him a withering look. 'It's at least three days' ride to the closest town and they wouldn't smell too good by then. We plant them here and save the government the cost of their funerals.'

'The ground's mighty hard around here,' Passlow argued. 'We won't be able to bury them very deep. What if the wolves and coyotes dig them up and scatter their bones everywhere?'

All the better, thought Glynn, but he replied, 'No self-respecting scavenger would want to eat this crew. Let's get them buried. The President himself will be waiting to hear how we handled this crew.'

Passlow was awe-struck. 'You mean that the President has been relying on us? What was so important about those killers?'

Glynn adopted a secretive air. 'I can't say too much because I'm sworn to secrecy but this was a matter of national importance. If you are asked just say that you are not allowed to discuss this matter. By now Washington knows the name of every man in this posse and if secrets start leaking out there'll be hell to pay. I'm the only member of this party authorized to speak and I'll supply the answers when the time comes.'

'What do we do about Bilney?' a man asked.

'We can't take him back with us. Bury him separate and deeper. Mark the spot well in case he has folks who want to collect the body later.'

All we need now is a town with a telegraph line and a newspaper, the marshal thought. The sight of a wounded leader and his heroic little band would attract attention and the name of Henry Glynn would leak out. Given the way stories became exaggerated as they were retold he imagined that the account of his battle would be suitably impressive by the time it reached Washington.

At last the wagons were rolling again and Kelly rode a fair way ahead, selecting areas best suited for wheels. Southern spurs of the Wolf Mountains forced them to travel out on the flatter ground but they were making slow westerly progress.

In places they were obliged to halt and dig down banks of arroyos so that the wagons could cross, backbreaking work but lightened by the knowledge that they were getting closer to Buffalo Creek. When he found an arroyo that could not be avoided, Kelly would wait there and assist in digging down the banks.

All were wondering how Glynn's posse had fared but with the hills between them, they knew not to expect the sound of gunshots.

For the third time that day Kelly and the Mayne boys were attacking a red clay arroyo bank when Ollie said, 'I wonder how that jackass lawman got on.'

Norton levered up a lump of hard-baked clay. He panted with the effort before throwing it aside. 'I don't care all that much. They're not helping get us to Buffalo Creek.'

'Maybe not,' Kelly agreed, 'but if they clean up that nest of renegades, life will he much safer for us later. That bunch were dangerous enough but if they were also meeting the Comanches in this area things could get mighty serious for anyone trying to make an honest living.'

Norton shifted a bit more dirt and paused for breath again. 'What about the Comanches? Do you think they'll keep coming back?'

'They might for a while but eventually the army will corral them on treaty land somewhere. History's against them. They'll fight for a while and I can't say I blame them, but now that the war's over, there are a lot more white folks heading west. This won't be Comanche country for much longer.'

By sundown the wagons obviously were not going to reach their objective so the travellers found an area with some grass and water and camped again.

Before they settled down for the night, Anna and Joe walked to a low ridge and looked westward.

Kelly pointed to the sloping end of the mountains that stood so darkly against the star-studded sky. 'That's the end of the Wolf Mountains. Travis told me that Buffalo Creek is the first big creek past where those hills end. Our two ranches must be only a couple of miles away now.'

FOURTEEN

The camp was astir early. This was the day that they would finally reach their new homes. Breakfast was hasty and they were soon on their way.

The country improved as they went, with more grassland and less rock and cactus.

Cattle tracks were everywhere and several times they saw distant groups of wild longhorns that trotted away into the rough country at the sight of the intruders.

'The place is already well-stocked with cattle,' Joe said, as he reined in his horse beside the leading wagon. 'And I think there are the remains of an old wagon trail up ahead. We're getting close.' He pointed across the flat ground to a dark line of trees that indicated a substantial water course. 'If the description that Travis gave me is right, that should be Buffalo Creek.'

'We'll make camp at the best place we find,' Mayne told him, 'and then take a ride around finding our boundaries. I have a list of ours here.'

'Travis wrote ours down as well. He knew where they were but he copied them off the title deeds for me too, just in case we got separated. As things turned out, it was lucky he did. His folks had a full section on the west bank of Buffalo Creek but he said that not much of it was fenced. They mostly ran the cattle on the open range but had a couple of pastures for horses. Heaven only knows the state of the fences that are there after three years of being abandoned.'

'Our ranch is the same size and has the ruins of an adobe house on its north end,' Mayne said. 'I'm hoping we can get a roof on it.'

'The ranches must be side-by-side.' Kelly liked that idea. 'I thought Travis said his folks were the only settlers, but he was away for years and there were probably others. His folks couldn't write and he didn't get much news from them when he was at the war.'

Ethel looked down from her seat beside Dan. 'What happened to his parents?'

'I think he said that the Comanches got them but they had everything tied up nice and legal for him and the will and deeds were held by their lawyer in Bondsville.'

'That was smart of them,' Dan observed.

'Travis was the same way. He tied up our partnership all nice and legal-like with the lawyer in Bondsville. Under the terms of the agreement, the whole place will belong to me now. Its a lousy way to come into a ranch though.'

As they approached Buffalo Creek, the overgrown wagon trail became more obvious and the teams found easier hauling.

Anna and Ollie had pushed ahead with the spare animals and were watering them at the stream when Kelly caught up with them. The creek was broad but shallow with a stony bottom, a reliable water source that would remain through the driest times. A line of flood debris about fifty yards from the water showed how much it had spread when in flood.

On a rise well back from the creek and screened by pecan trees, the ruins of an adobe building could just be discerned among the greenery.

'That's the ruin that Hannan told us about,' Ollie said. 'Looks like we hit the right spot at last.'

'It might not be,' Kelly told him. 'There's an adobe ruin on my place too. There could be another somewhere downstream. According to the details that Travis copied from the ranch deeds, the northern boundary is marked by a cairn of stones about fifty yards north of the house. From there it runs straight west for a mile to some hills where there is another marker. The boundary runs south then for a mile and comes back on to the creek. Lets go across and see if we can locate that marker. It should tell us which of the ranches it is.'

The wagons reached the ford just after the others had crossed.

'The bottom's sound,' Ollie called. 'Come across.'

As Dan shook the reins and urged the team into the water, he turned in his seat and kissed Ethel on the cheek. 'There you are, my girl. The ranch we have finally managed to buy.'

The spare stock were grazing on the grassy flat and the three riders were looking about the ruin when the wagons pulled up. Dan jumped down and began to unhitch the team while Ethel walked across to inspect the old house. But she did not go too close. The roof had fallen in and there was a good chance of encountering a snake among the overgrown shrubs that surrounded the building. 'I think we will need to build a new house,' she told her husband.

Anna rode across to her parents. 'This might not be our ranch. Joe says that it fits the description that Travis copied from the title deeds for his ranch. He won't know for sure until he can find all the boundary markers but thinks that our place might he about a mile to the south.'

Dan was not worried. 'Let's eat first. Then I'll take a horse and Joe and I can check the boundaries. I have a description written by Hannan so we can compare notes and soon figure out who owns what.'

Norton was first to finish his meal and started exploring on foot. A short while later, he called to the others. 'I've found a corner marker. It's over here in the long grass.'

'That should give us a starting point,'

Kelly said.

Dan saddled a horse and pointing their mounts' heads to the west, they rode toward the distant hills. Not far from the ruins they saw the charred remains of corrals. Kelly pointed to it. 'Travis said there were corrals behind the house. Looks like the Comanches burned them while he was away.'

'Hannan never mentioned any corrals,' Mayne said. 'This could be your spread.'

They rode on and had no trouble locating the western-most marker. It was cut into the trunk of a huge pine. Kelly looked straight to the south. 'That agrees with what Travis wrote, but finding the next marker might not be so easy. There are a fair few trees down that way. Unless we can judge the distance to an exact mile, we could be looking in the wrong place. The marker is supposed to be carved on a small post planted in the ground.'

Dan looked worried. 'According to my directions, our western marker should be a pine tree marked like this one. If our spreads are adjoining, my north-western marker should also be your south-western marker. Something's wrong here, Joe.'

'Maybe the two places aren't exactly side by side,' Kelly suggested. 'There might he another homestead claim in between.'

It took them nearly all hour to locate the next marker and it was a weathered post as Kelly had expected.

'That settles it,' Dan announced. 'Let's ride straight east and pick up your final marker on the creek. Then we can ride downstream and see if we can find the second ruined adobe house. It shouldn't be far away.'

Eventually they found Kelly's last marker, another cairn of stones. 'That's the right place for sure,' the younger man said. 'Fits exactly with the description copied from the deeds.'

'Unfortunately, it also agrees with the boundaries that Hannan gave us,' Dan sounded very worried. 'Something's wrong here. We both seem to be looking at the same piece of ground, except yours was owned by a family named Travis.'

'Travis was my partner's first name,' Kelly corrected. 'The family name was Neal.'

Dan went pale. 'We bought our place through a land agent named Hannan as a deceased estate from a family called Neal. We are both laying claim to the same piece of ground. Now I know why that conniving skunk deliberately gave us wrong directions. He did not want us meeting up with you or your partner. We have one hell of a problem here.'

'I reckon that problem is Hannan's. I wonder how many times he has sold this ranch.'

'If that's the case, Joe, what happened to the folks who bought it?'

'I think it's about time we found out.'

Henry Glynn, with his wounded arm in a sling, tried to look heroic as he led his men down the main street of Bondsville. Bilney's riderless horse added a suitably dramatic touch. Outside the office of the *Bondsville Bugle* he sagged weakly in his saddle like a man at the end of his endurance.

Walter Holly, the paper's editor, had watched the procession through his window and now, as Glynn had hoped, rushed out with pencil and notebook. The marshal's badge pinned to his vest and the blood-stained bandage around his arm advertised that the lawman had a story to tell. Holly hurried to where Glynn had halted his horse and introduced himself before asking what had happened.

Glynn had mentally rehearsed this scene a hundred times. 'I can't say too much unless I am authorized from Washington, but these men here' – he pointed to the posse as he spoke – 'have made the United States a safer place to live. We had a battle, but three men who murdered a government agent in Mexico are now dead. The killers were on Texas soil but we got them before they could kill anyone else.'

Holly was suitably impressed. 'Don't give

all the credit to your men, Marshal. You surely must have been leading the fight. How else did you get that wound?'

'I cut myself shaving,' Glynn said, aware that his casual response would make good reading later. 'I would like to help you, Mr Holly, but first I must report to your local lawman, send a telegram to Washington and see to my men and horses. After I get this wound dressed I am prepared to give you an interview although there is much that I won't be able to tell you without the President's permission.'

Holly saw the foundations of a good story and knew how to mix facts, guesswork and downright lies. He knew he could do wonders with a little information. 'Of course, Marshal, duty comes first. I'll call on you in a couple of hours' time.'

Trying to conceal his elation, Glynn straightened in his saddle and set his mount into motion. 'Forward, men,' he said in a weak voice. 'Soon we can rest.'

The red-haired man turned to Passlow.

'Why is he suddenly so tired? We had a good rest last night and we've only come five miles today.'

Passlow had Glynn figured, but decided that hitching his wagon to his boss's star might have certain advantages. 'Shut up,' he growled. 'Marshal Glynn knows what he's doing.'

FIFTEEN

It seemed as if a barrier had descended between the Mayne family and Kelly. Suddenly they were competing for the same piece of ground. There was no open resentment or hostility of any kind, but both parties unconsciously blamed the other for spoiling their dreams.

'There's only one thing to do,' Kelly said, as they finished a rather awkward meal together that night. 'We have to go back to

Bondsville and sort out this mess. Will you come with me, Dan?'

Mayne rubbed a hand across his forehead. 'Maybe that would be best,' he said, after a delay of several seconds. 'But I don't like leaving Ethel and the kids out here alone.'

'Don't worry,' Norton told him. 'The army's chased away the Comanches and Marshal Glynn has no doubt cleared out that gang of renegades. It is probably safer here than it's been for years.'

Ethel looked worried. 'I'm not sure that Glynn could clear out anything. But it is important that we find out where we stand. You really need to go, Dan. Every cent we ever saved is tied up in this ranch.'

'How long do you reckon the return trip should take us, Joe?'

'Four – maybe five days, depending on what we find when we get to town.'

'Good. Let's get an early start in the morning.'

Cedric Hannan was loath to leave Bonds-

151

ville until he had to. Though only in his late twenties he had done well in the town, rising from a clerk's job in a law office to his own real estate business. If he could weather the current crisis, he would soon be a wealthy man. But if matters looked to be getting too hot he had packed saddle-bags near his desk and a fast horse in the stable behind his premises.

Slight in build and unassuming in manner, the young man with the wispy, fair hair looked nothing like the criminal he had become. The idea first came to him in the law office where he saw title deeds held in trust for men who would never return from the Civil War. Several times he had sold the Neal ranch on Buffalo Creek but the purchasers had never gained final control of the deeds. These would be held back on the pretence of legal formalities and the unsuspecting buyers would be directed into the clutches of Preston and the others, or occasionally, when Cherokee could arrange it, a Comanche war party. Buffalo Creek was considered to be Comanche country and few asked questions when would-be buyers disappeared. They took a chance. What did they expect? Some loot was exchanged with the Comanches and periodically a pack train would arrive to take away what could be sold in another district.

A fairly simple plan became complicated when Travis Neal returned to claim his heritage and a hard-riding messenger was sent to alert the renegades. He had been told later that Neal was dead, but then heard by accident from his former employer that he had sold a half share in the ranch. Fortunately he had misdirected the Mayne family straight toward the renegades' camp and had not been worried about Neal's partner until Cherokee spurred his exhausted horse into Bondsville late at night. The news that the renegades had been swooped on by a posse took him completely by surprise. What if some were captured and talked? He knew that Neal was dead, but the Maynes had survived. Kelly and the

Mayne family would almost certainly meet at Buffalo Creek and questions would soon be asked.

The sight of Glynn's posse arriving without prisoners gave Hannan a glimmer of hope. Later when he heard that the renegades had all died fighting, he knew that the situation could still be saved. Until the Maynes and Kelly met, his deception would not be discovered. If both parties could be eliminated, it would be a case of business as usual. He was wondering who he could recruit to remove the troublesome parties when Cherokee walked boldly into his office.

Momentarily Hannan was lost for words but then he hissed, 'Cherokee, what in the hell are you doing here? Don't you know the lawman that got the others is in town?'

It was not often that the half-breed smiled, but he flashed his teeth in a happy grin. 'Don't you know? The word's all over town. That jackass lawman thinks he killed three outlaws from Mexico. He planted our boys under the wrong names. There's nothing to connect them with us.'

Hannan could scarcely believe his luck. His plans soared again. 'Would you be able to round up a few men, Cherokee?'

'How many?'

'Three or four.'

'Maybe.' A note of suspicion crept into Cherokee's voice. 'What's the job?'

'There are people out on Buffalo Creek on the south side of the Wolf Mountains. They'll be heading this way soon, might even be on the way. I want them killed.'

'What's it worth?'

'I'll pay fifty dollars per man and supply any ammunition or provisions you need plus an extra fifty dollars for every man killed.'

'How many are we up against?'

'I reckon two or three at first. They need to be stopped straight away. There'll be others at Buffalo Creek and we can do a similar deal, but that comes later. How does that sound?'

Cherokees dark eyes narrowed. 'Make my

payment a hundred for every killing and you have a deal.'

Hannan was in no mood to argue. Time was precious. He took a hundred dollars in notes from his desk drawer and passed the money across. 'Take this for expenses. I want you and your men out of town today. Those people from Buffalo Creek must not get past you.'

Happy was helping to shoe horses for the trail drive north when one of the drovers returned from Bondsville. He was working with the remuda while Carstairs and Machin had gone with the rest of the crew to collect the cattle that they would take to Kansas.

'Big news in town today,' the man announced, as he dismounted and hitched his horse to the side of the chuck wagon.

Happy looked up from the hoof he was rasping. 'Did someone get hisself shot?'

'Not in town but a posse just came in. They killed three outlaws. They didn't say much at first but some were in the saloon later and let a few things slip after a whiskey or two. Story is these characters were wanted for killing some American official in Mexico. The President himself was taking a personal interest in the affair – or so someone said.'

'Any idea who those dead fellers were?'

'I heard the names. One was called Carmody or Carstairs, something like that. But I can't recall the others. They were supposed to be ex-rebs who'd been in Mexico fighting with Maximilian, that Austrian duke.'

'And the marshal got the lot of them?'

The man nodded. 'That's what I heard. They're dead and buried. The marshal found a lot of loot in their camp too. Sounds like they needed killing real bad. But they won't ever be a problem again.'

Sure won't, Happy told himself. Living would be a lot easier for the three of them now they were officially dead.

SIXTEEN

The departure from the camp at Buffalo Creek was a strained process with Kelly feeling very much an outsider. Though the Mayne family wished him luck he knew that they had hoped his luck did not extend to ownership of the ranch. He drew some consolation from the fact that Anna seemed genuinely sorry to see him go.

'I hope you and Pa can get this mess straightened out,' she told him. 'We were all so pleased when we thought we would be neighbours. You're practically part of the family now.'

'You be careful while I'm gone, Anna. This is still dangerous country. I'd hate anything to happen to you. I'll be back in a few days but till then, be careful.'

'I've survived nineteen years without your

protection, Joe Kelly,' she teased. 'I think I'll last a little longer.'

'Make sure you do,' he said quietly, as he mounted his horse. 'There's no guarantee that Glynn caught up with all those renegades. If any escaped they could head this way. Stay close to camp and don't go anywhere without a gun.'

They were travelling light with a single blanket apiece and enough food in their saddle-bags for two days on the trail. Neither man wanted to be burdened with a pack animal. As their horses splashed across the ford Dan twisted in his saddle and looked back. 'That's a nice piece of ground,' he said regretfully. The implication that one of them would be the loser was left unsaid.

The morning was cool and fresh and the horses stepped out energetically. It was early enough for wildlife to be moving about and they disturbed a few deer and the odd rabbit. At one stage a red fox ran silently up a hill at their approach and paused briefly to look back when partially concealed in a patch of ferns.

They encountered cattle too, small groups on the way to the creek that scattered and went crashing through the brush upon sighting the riders.

'There are plenty of cattle,' Kelly observed. 'But it will be hell's own work getting them out of the brush and getting brands on them.'

'At the few dollars a head they're worth in Texas, it will take a lot of cattle to make much of a profit,' Dan said.

'There's a trail herder named Chisholm opened a new trail north and if stories are right, Texas cattle are bringing good money in Kansas, so the cattle business here is likely to pick up.'

'Kansas is an almighty long way from here,' the older man growled.

Henry Glynn planned to remain in Bondsville long enough to pay off his men, ply them, with liquor and guarantee that the supposedly secret battle against their country's enemies was publicized widely. Then he wrote a lengthy report that he had to copy by hand and send to his superiors along with cuttings from the *Bondsville Bugle*. Apart from the names of the wrongly identified dead men, he ensured that his was the only other name mentioned.

Hannan could not believe his luck. He even dared to venture into the saloon and listen to Passlow's account of the battle that became more and more exaggerated with each telling. The more that drunken posse members confused the true situation, the better it suited him. On the strength of that he even bought Glynn's lieutenant a drink that was hardly beneficial to his powers of recollection.

If Cherokee and his men successfully way-laid anyone approaching from the direction of Buffalo Creek, Cedric Hannan's worries were over. He had seen the half-breed leaving town with three men who had rather dubious reputations around the town. One, who called himself Bill Brown, was reputed to be handy with a gun but Saunders and Oulton, the other pair, were just local thugs. When opponents were small enough, or drunk enough, they might engage in a bit of bar-room brawling but neither was particularly noted for courage. The latter quality though was superfluous when shooting unsuspecting men from ambush. Hannan had no reason to doubt that his hirelings could handle the task he had set them.

With a day of shoeing horses behind him, Happy was also easing his aching back while gathering information for his friends. The trail herd would be arriving in the vicinity of Bondsville the following day and the long journey north would begin. Carstairs and Machin, now known as Curtis and Marlowe, would he greatly relieved when he told them the news.

Glynn appeared briefly at the batwing doors of the saloon but saw that Passlow was doing what he had hoped and retired quietly before he was noticed by the drinkers. But ever watchful, Happy saw him and his eyes narrowed in anger. This man had intended to kill them on sight, just as he had the renegades. It took all his self-control to stop from following the marshal in the hope that he would stray too close to a dark alley. But then he realized that he would be foolish to jeopardize the chance of a normal life again. Henry Glynn never knew how lucky he was.

Kelly and Dan halted in the late afternoon at a spot where they had camped previously on the inward journey. There was grass, water and firewood. Their hobbled horses would be less likely to stray when on a patch of good feed.

The travellers could have made a few more miles before darkness set in but would not have found as good a campsite. They could easily regain lost time tomorrow when the horses were fresh and their path was easy to see.

After setting up camp and a meal they had brought from Buffalo Creek, the pair set out to discuss their dilemma seriously.

'Travis never mentioned this Hannan character,' Kelly said. 'As far as I know all his dealings were with a lawyer named Hamilton. I remember we signed a few papers in his office, a little feller he was, had a gammy leg from the war. Did you have any dealings with him?'

'No. Our dealings were all with Hannan. Said he was a land agent acting on behalf of a deceased estate that had to he sold because of back taxes. He said that the title deeds were with Hamilton being fixed up, but had written down all the details of the ranch. I paid him a thousand bucks and got a receipt and I was to come back to Bondsville in six weeks' time to finalize the paperwork with the lawyer. To date the only paperwork I have is Hannan's receipt, and a written description of the ranch. The rest was all in Hamilton's hands.'

Kelly reminded him, 'You have one more piece of paper. Hannan also gave you a hand-drawn map that would have steered you straight into a bunch of murderous renegades if the Comanches didn't get you first. It seems that the renegades knew Travis was on his way, but they didn't seem to know about me.'

'So you reckon Hannan's behind this?'

'He has to be. Hamilton knew of our partnership agreement and if he was up to monkey business, would have sent his men after me. He knew I would inherit everything if Travis died. Hannan had all the details of the deed, but did not have the deed itself. He did not know about the change in ownership.'

Dan sounded far from happy. 'So you think I have no legal claim to the ranch?'

'To be honest, it looks that way, but the law is a strange thing and I could be wrong. Let's wait till we hear what Hamilton and Hannan have to say about all this.'

'If I lose that ranch I'm going to get my money back out of someone's hide. You can be sure of that.'

Cherokee had taken his men in a wide

detour to avoid being sighted by members of the ever-vigilant Rutledge clan. He knew where their lookouts were and was taking no chances. Only when they were safe from observation did they settle down for the night. They were on the tracks left by the wagons and Glynn's posse and had no doubt that their intended victims would be travelling by the same route albeit in the reverse direction.

Only Cherokee was used to outdoor living and he had to drive his reluctant henchmen to collect firewood and set up a most rudimentary camp. They were not particularly interested in eating at that stage but were keen to attack the supply of liquor they had brought from town. As he secured the horses and looked to their welfare, the half-breed found it hard to disguise his disgust. These men were the bottom of the criminal barrel but he knew that they would serve their purpose if he led them properly. If a couple should contract fatal doses of lead poisoning while performing their tasks, the venture could still end up a success for him. He intended moving on as soon as Hannan paid him. The organization was starting to fall apart and he wanted to be long gone when the law took a long-belated hand in matters.

The gang were imbibing freely by the time that sleep became necessary but they showed a distinct reluctance to move away from the fire and stretch out on the hard ground.

'If any of you sonsofbitches has the sense of a gopher,' Cherokee told them, 'you'll turn in now. We have an early start in the morning and you'll be sick as dogs. I'm telling you now: I'll shoot any man who won't get out of his blankets tomorrow.'

'What's so special about tomorrow?' Oulton demanded.

Brown was also drunk enough to argue. 'This Mayne *hombre* or the other one we're supposed to be looking for could take a week at least before they head for town. You're worrying too much.'

Cherokee did not agree. His narrow escape

from Glynn's posse had left him with a much greater degree of caution. 'They could be here as early as tomorrow morning and we have to find a good place to dry-gulch them. If we don't get the right place, some of us could get hurt or one of them might get away. We can't afford to be careless.'

'I can handle them,' Brown said confidently.

Oulton supported him. 'They won't know what hit them. Stop worrying.'

Saunders had not bought into the argument. He had lapsed into a drunken slumber.

Their leader felt far from reassured. It was logical that most of the Mayne family would remain at Buffalo Creek but if they all decided to confront Hannan, he would have to wipe out three armed men and two women who might also have guns. He was not sure whether Kelly would be with them and, if he was, the ambushers would be outnumbered. Brown might give a good account of himself but he was not sure of how much he could count on the other pair if a bit of lead started coming back at them. In the morning he would have to find an ambush site that was sure to tip the balance in his favour, no matter how many they had to fight.

Cherokee removed his boots and gunbelt, arranged a holstered revolver close at hand and rolled himself in his blanket. The next few hours would present him with few worries but when day broke things could be very different.

SEVENTEEN

Cherokee woke his men early and was greeted with groans reflecting everything from extreme agony to rage at being disturbed. It was no use appealing to their better sides; he doubted they had any. Instead he tried to imbue them with a sense of urgency. 'Come on, fellers. You don't want them Buffalo Creek jaspers to catch you in your blankets.'

'They probably ain't even left Buffalo Creek,' Oulton protested. 'They couldn't get here so early in the day.'

Saunders favoured a more direct approach to the problem. 'Go away.'

'I'm dying,' Brown announced.

'Serves you right. I warned you what would happen if you sat up half the night drinking that rotgut. Now get out of those blankets, you ornery skunks, and start earning your money. We don't know when those others will be along and we haven't found a place to tie up and wait for them yet. Now, get moving.'

Brown glared from bloodshot eyes. 'I don't take orders from some dirty, no-good 'breed.' As he spoke, he reached toward the holstered gun on the ground beside him.

But Cherokee was not easily bluffed. 'You'll take orders from me because the way you are at present, you couldn't hit your finger if it was shoved down the barrel. If that gun looks anywhere near pointing in my direction, I'll kill you. I'm calling your bluff, Bill. Do as I say or go for that gun. I'm in a hurry so make up your mind.'

Something about Cherokee's attitude told Brown that co-operation would be more beneficial to his health than confrontation. 'Keep your shirt on,' he mumbled as he reached for his boots. 'There's no point in us killing each other.'

'Glad you see my point of view. Let's get eating – those who can – and then we'll pack up and get out of here.'

Kelly and Mayne had started earlier and saw the smoke from Cherokee's camp-fire rising from behind a tree-covered spur of the mountains a couple of miles to the east.

Kelly pointed to the thin column of smoke. 'We're not alone.'

'You reckon it's Indians?'

'They wouldn't be so careless as to have a fire alight in daylight unless it was for signalling, and there's no sign of that.'

'What about the Rutledge family?'

'There's no need for them to camp out. They're not all that far from home and none of their cattle is running on this side of the mountains. It might be Marshal Glynn lost or looking for some of those renegades who might have got away.'

'What about those three rebs?'

'They wouldn't be hanging around here when they had fresh horses.'

With a sour expression on his face, Mayne suggested, 'Maybe it's some other poor sucker who has just bought a ranch on Buffalo Creek.'

Something suddenly stirred Kelly's memory. 'I was wondering where I had heard Hannan's name before just came to me. When I has hiding near Travis Neal's body, I heard the killers who came looking for him mention Hannan's name. They were working for him. That's why they killed Travis. They didn't know about our partnership.'

An angry tone crept into Mayne's voice.

'That little skunk deliberately steered us the wrong way with that map. He wanted us to run into those killers.'

'Or the Comanches. I think that both lots were acting in cahoots. If one didn't get you the other would.'

'I'm going to tear that coyote's liver out with my bare hands when I meet him.'

'Right now,' Kelly said, 'I'm more interested in meeting those who are up ahead. But I think we should see them before they see us. While we can see that smoke we'll know they're still in camp. When that fire goes out though, I reckon we should find a nice safe spot and watch the wagon trail. If they're up to no good, they'll stick to your wheel tracks.'

Kelly had forgotten that a spur of the mountain covered in tall pines would cut out his view for some time. When they rounded the spur there was no smoke in the sky. 'That fire's out,' he told Mayne, 'so the ones who made it are probably on the move and we can't be sure how long they've been

173

travelling. Keep your eyes peeled. We might be mighty close to them.'

'There's always the chance that they're travelling in the same direction as us. If that's the case they could stay ahead of us.'

'Don't bet your life on it, Dan. I have a feeling that those *hombres* up ahead will not be friends of ours.'

The brush was thick at the base of the mountains and consequently visibility was limited. It was a situation that Kelly did not like and it made him nervous. He rode in silence with every sense alert. His bay horse was a better walker than Mayne's mount and was about a horse length ahead when they rode to the edge of the trees facing an open patch of ground. He was about to cross it when, from the trees on the other side, he heard a horse snort. 'Trouble,' he said softly to Mayne.

Simultaneously, Cherokee and his riders appeared on the other side of the clearing. Momentarily both parties reined up in surprise.

Kelly recognized the half-breed from the day he had found his partner's body. His right hand flew to the butt of the Whitney on his right hip.

Cherokee would have retreated but the riders behind him prevented that. Left with no other option, he too went for his gun.

Kelly had been forewarned and was just that much quicker and he used the slight time advantage to aim more carefully. Unfortunately, Mayne's horse bumped into his own mount's rump as he was squeezing the trigger. The bullet that should have hit Cherokee dead centre ploughed a furrow along the renegade's ribs instead.

With an angry snarl, the half-breed fired back, but his horse, too, was moving and the shot went wide. The frightened horse swung to the right giving Kelly a side-on shot at its rider. This time he did not miss. The bullet took the half-breed in the side and knocked him from his saddle.

Brown was next in line and Mayne tried a shot but the cap misfired. As he frantically recocked his revolver, Oulton sent a shot in his direction. The near miss from his new adversary slightly distracted Mayne and he hesitated before sending another shot Brown's way. It nearly cost him his life. Brown's Navy Colt barked viciously and Mayne crumpled forward in his saddle.

Kelly snapped a shot at Brown and scored a hit. He saw his target reel and drop his gun. As the wounded man sought to turn his mount out of the battle, Mayne came back into the fight and dropped Oulton from his horse. By this time Saunders, who was hindmost, had wheeled his pony about and was fleeing the scene. Another shot from an enraged Mayne sent the fleeing man on his way, terrified but unscathed.

'Let him go,' Kelly called, 'but watch the others.'

The warning was timely as Brown was dragging himself across the ground to reach for a fallen weapon. Mayne, still hunched over and gasping for breath, was in no mood to give warnings or show mercy. He fired two shots into the would-be killer who never moved again.

While keeping a wary eye on the other two fallen gunmen, Kelly asked, 'How badly are you hit, Dan?'

'This is my lucky day. The bullet glanced off my saddle horn and was deflected into my belt. It hit a double fold of heavy leather and didn't go through into me. I bet I'll have a hell of a bruise there though.'

'You're lucky he wasn't using a .44 because it might just have gone through.'

'Damned gun misfired on me, too,' the older man complained.

'That's always been a problem with these cap-and-ball revolvers. You will always get a few misfires. That's why I carry two.' Kelly dismounted as he spoke. 'Keep an eye out for trouble while I try to find something out about our friends here.'

Cherokee was dead, his face distorted in a grimace of pain or shock. He carried no identification. 'I know this coyote was one of those who shot Travis Neal but I don't know who he is.'

'Don't worry about him,' Mayne said. 'We'll let the law in Bondsville find out that detail. We know now that they were after us.'

'I also know that this one worked for Hannan. It looks like he's behind all this.'

Kelly continued to search the other dead men. He found Brown's name inside his hat but Oulton had no identification. Finally he straightened up and walked to his horse. 'I reckon we need to get on that last skunk's trail and try to catch him before he tells some lying story to the law.'

'What about these bodies?'

'Leave them. The quicker we get to Bondsville, the better.'

Saunders rode hard, too hard for the inferior animal that he bestrode. Panic had taken over from the slight knowledge of horsemanship that he possessed. Two miles from the scene of the shooting, the animal was winded and its pace slowed dramatically. By much kicking and lashing of rein ends he kept his mount moving but its stumbling trot quickly became a plodding walk. Fearfully he kept twisting in his saddle looking for signs of pursuit and after an hour was relieved to see no sign of anyone on his trail. He was not to know that his pursuers had set off at a much steadier pace that their horses could hold without exhausting themselves. It would take another hour for them to catch him. Bondsville was still many miles away. Wishful thinking had replaced panic and now Saunders was beginning to think that there would be no pursuit. He had seen Mayne hit and reached the conclusion that Kelly had stayed behind to help the wounded man. Having deluded himself, he halted to rest his horse.

Dismounting, he eased the cinches on his saddle and stood there beside the sweat-drenched animal as it stood with drooping head. Saunders was basically a townsman and unaccustomed to long hours in the saddle. As the horse rested, he walked about in an effort to get the stiffness out of his legs. Then, after about a fifteen-minute rest, he tightened the cinches again and re-mounted. The horse was too weary to keep up a decent pace and it required hard work to keep it moving at all, but the rider knew that he had to make the best time possible. He was debating in his mind what he would tell Hannan, or whether he should even go near the land agent, and had forgotten to look behind him. A glance over his shoulder would have shown him that two riders were now within half a mile of him.

'It don't look like he's seen us yet,' Mayne said.

'Won't matter now if he does. Look at his horse tracks. That pony of his hasn't got a gallop left in it by the way it's dragging its feet.'

They topped a rise and suddenly Kelly stood in his stirrups and pointed ahead. 'There's our man.'

EIGHTEEN

Saunders eventually looked back after he had been riding for a while and was shocked to see the two riders behind him. They had narrowed the gap between them to about 300 yards. Already they were in rifle range. He drove his heels into his mount's sides and lashed it again with the rein ends. The horse responded as best it could, breaking into a slow lumbering gallop.

The hunters' mounts also jumped into a gallop and were closing on Saunders rapidly. Soon the fugitive gunman could hear hoofs pounding behind him. He glanced back. The younger rider on the bay horse had drawn his carbine and had it to his shoulder with the barrel supported across the forearm of his bridle hand.

'Stop,' Kelly called. 'I'll start shooting if

181

you don't.'

Knowing that his position was hopeless. Saunders hauled back on his reins and raised his right hand to show that he was not holding a weapon. His weary pony was only too pleased to halt. It stood there with sides heaving, a picture of exhaustion as the pursuers galloped up.

The Ball carbine in Kelly's hands was a short weapon but its .50 calibre bore was most intimidating when viewed from the front.

'Don't shoot. I give up.'

'Get off that horse and keep your hands up,' Kelly ordered. 'Don't try going for your gun because you won't make it.'

'I know that,' Saunders's admitted sullenly. 'Why are you after me?'

Mayne growled, 'Blame it on the company you keep. There are a few questions that need answering and if you give the right answers you might just stay alive.'

'I didn't know the others would start shooting – honest.'

'You and honesty parted company a long time ago.' Mayne's voice grew more menacing. 'Now, you'll start giving us straight answers, or you can join the rest of your friends. Your first lie will be your last words.'

'While that horse of yours is getting its wind back, we are going to have a long talk. Just unbuckle your gunbelt and be careful about it,' Kelly said.

Saunders was scared and talked freely. He disclosed that he had been recruited by Cherokee who was working on Hannan's behalf. He knew little of the half-breed's activities or the killings performed by the renegades at Hannan's request. By his own admission he was only a petty criminal who had taken the job because of the money offered. With the renegade gang's destruction Cherokee did not have a very large pool of likely recruits. Normally he would not have considered Saunders but had reasoned that there was strength in numbers.

'I told you the truth,' the prisoner said nervously. 'Now what happens to me?'

Mayne thought for a while and then said, 'If you tell the same to the law in Bondsville, I think you'll get off pretty lightly. As far as we know you did not fire at either of us, and we're prepared to say that.'

Kelly added, 'But if you change your story when we get to town, I'll hunt you down no matter how long it takes. Let's get on our horses now. It's a long ride to town.'

The hero of the Wolf Mountains battle was celebrating his last night in Bondsville. Tomorrow he was returning to his home base in Austin by stagecoach.

The townspeople had found Glynn interesting in small doses but his self-promotion was beginning to wear thin. Some were wondering how the United States had been saved from a gang of ruthless but unknown killers from Mexico when details were so vague and the secrecy that the marshal often invoked aroused more curiosity than it satisfied.

Hannan had been one of the few who

seemed to enjoy Glynn's company, but this was because he was trying to bolster his image as a law-abiding citizen. He was relying on Cherokee to remove permanently the embarrassment of irate settlers arriving from Buffalo Creek, but in case things went wrong, he saw certain advantages in having friends among lawmen. And a friend with influence that reached all the way to Washington could prove to be a powerful ally. Accordingly, he was prepared to listen to yet another version of the famous battle that only Glynn had seen. The rest of his posse had returned to their homes and anonymity.

'I suppose you'll find life pretty quiet in Austin now that those killers have been cleaned out.' He poured Glynn another drink as he spoke.

'I expect so,' the marshal replied. 'But chances are I'll be called back East on some other special assignment.' He sincerely believed that his career would be boosted considerably when his report arrived in Washington.

Hannan imparted a note of admiration into his voice. 'I envy you, Henry. Selling land in a small town is not the most exciting job in the world, but I suppose some of us are not cut out for the adventurous life. I'm not sure that I would be very good at dodging bullets. You can have the exciting life,' he said, oblivious of the excitement heading his way.

NINETEEN

It was nearly midnight by the time Kelly and Mayne reached town with their prisoner. Jack Burton, the deputy sheriff, was about to lock the office for the night when the three horsemen halted outside.

'Are you the sheriff?' Mayne asked.

'I'm his deputy. Name's Burton. Sheriff Cahill will be on duty tomorrow morning. Can I help?'

While the prisoner sat silently on his horse, the other two explained about the gun battle and its fatal results. The deputy listened in amazement and when the account was finished, he asked Saunders, 'Do you agree with what these men are saying?'

After nervously licking his lips, he replied, 'That's right. But I didn't know that Cherokee was planning to murder anyone. He said he was settling a personal score and needed a bit of help.'

'Tell him who hired Cherokee,' Mayne prompted.

'He said Hannan hired him – Hannan's the one behind this mess.'

'I was wanting to talk to Sheriff Cahill anyway,' Mayne said, 'about some land deals at Buffalo Creek that Hannan is behind.'

'And we need to talk to that lawyer,' Kelly added.

Deputy Burton gave a sigh of resignation and reopened the office door. 'I thought this would be an easy night and was going home early, but it looks like I'll have to wait for Sheriff Cahill to come on in the morning. I'll put Mr Saunders here in a cell and you pair are welcome to bunk down in the spare one. There's a corral behind the office where you can leave your horses. The livery stable is well and truly closed by now. I don't know where you would get anything to eat at this time of night, but I can make us all a cup of coffee.'

None was in the best of moods when they awoke in the morning and the sheriff was late starting work. Kelly and Mayne had a wash and presented themselves for a breakfast of ham and eggs at the local hotel while Burton arranged for a meal to be brought in for the prisoner.

Phil Hamilton was Bondsville's only lawyer and his office was opposite the hotel. Kelly and Mayne had just finished breakfast when they saw him opening his office. They wasted no time in confronting him. Hamilton was a slightly built man of about fifty with a permanent limp that had resulted from service in the Mexican War. He had spent much of his life on the frontier and was used to armed, none-too-clean customers but his instincts told him that the business of the pair before him would not be routine. After brief introductions, he indicated that they should seat themselves on the other side of his big desk. 'You look worried, gents. What can I do for you?'

Both men told him of their concerns. The lawyer frowned and went to a wooden cabinet. As he looked through various bundles of papers, he told them, 'I remember Travis Neal arranging a partnership deal fairly recently.' Withdrawing a cardboard folder, he said, 'I still have the deeds here. Neal left them here with me, the same as his folks used to.'

Mayne's voice was heavy with disappointment and anger. 'So there's no way that Hannan, the land agent, had access to these deeds?'

'He used to work for me before he went out on his own,' Hamilton explained. 'He had access to them then. We had several filed away waiting for their owners to come back from the war. Some have not been claimed yet and I doubt that they ever will, but without the permission of Travis Neal, Hannan had no right, to dispose of the property. If he took your money, Mr. Mayne, without the owner's permission, it is a case of fraud. I was secretly pleased when that man left my employment. He seemed to be showing a bit too much interest in other folks' business. Now I am beginning to understand why. I would suggest a word with Hannan to clarify the position and you should seriously consider bringing this matter to Sheriff Cahill's attention.'

Mayne stood up, his face flushed with rage. 'I'll have more than one word with that thieving little skunk and the sheriff is sure to find out when I shoot him full of holes. He not only stole a thousand dollars from me but he tried to steer my family the wrong way so that we'd be killed by Indians or renegades.' His angry outburst finished,

Mayne strode to the door.

'I'll go with him and try to keep him out of trouble,' Kelly said.

He had to run to catch up with his friend and caught him just as he was pushing through the door of Hannan's office which was only a few doors clown the street from the lawyer's. A sandy-haired young man behind a desk looked up in surprise as the pair entered. 'Can I help you gentlemen?'

'I doubt it,' Mayne rasped. 'But if you want to help yourself you have a few questions to answer.'

Hannan played for time. He had been sure that Cherokee and his men would have prevented the predicament in which he now found himself. It had not occurred to him that they might fail. 'Mr Mayne, isn't it? I hadn't expected to see you so soon. What seems to be the trouble?'

'The trouble is that you took a thousand dollars off me for a ranch that you had no power to sell.'

'I'm sure there's been a mix-up somewhere with the paperwork,' the young man said smoothly. 'If there is, I can arrange a refund of your money.'

'That ain't the half of it. You gave me a map that steered me and my family straight into the path of a Comanche war party. And if they missed us, there was a bunch of white renegades waiting.'

Kelly spoke for the first time. 'You also sent those same renegades out to kill Travis Neal. And you would have had them after me if you had known of the partnership arrangement I had with him.'

Hannan assumed a puzzled expression that looked almost convincing. 'I don't know of any renegades and Comanche raiders are always unpredictable. Sounds like there has been a big mistake somewhere.'

'The mistake is that one of them renegades is alive and is now at the sheriff's office,' Mayne told him.

The land agent remained unruffled. He knew he had no chance of drawing the short-barrelled revolver he carried under his coat. Cautiously he indicated a desk drawer. 'I'm not going for a gun,' he told them. 'There is a cash box in there and if Mr Mayne is unhappy with the deal that I might have mistakenly made, I am prepared to return his money. I have my good name to protect.' He extracted a roll of bills and counted out a thousand dollars.

'Here's your money back. Count it,' he said, as he passed the cash to Mayne.

'That's the easy bit, Kelly told him. 'Now there's the matter of a murder and several attempted murders. You're not off the hook yet, Hannan.'

To their surprise, the land agent shot both hands skywards and said urgently, 'Don't shoot – take all the money.'

With their backs to the window, neither Kelly nor Mayne saw Henry Glynn looking in from the street. He had been on his way to the stage station when he saw what appeared to be a hold-up in progress. His most ardent admirer, after himself, was standing there with arms raised and a terrified expression on his face.

Stealthily the marshal stepped through the door with a gun in his hand.

'Have you gone loco?' Mayne demanded of Hannan.

Kelly heard a sound behind him and half turned. Glynn slammed a gun barrel into his temple and dropped him to his knees. Almost in the same motion, he jammed the gun into Mayne's face. 'Don't move.'

Hannan was delighted. 'Good work, Henry. Keep them covered. I'll get Sheriff Cahill.' He snatched up the small cash box and ran past the lawman.

'Why in the hell did you do that?' Kelly demanded.

'That man's a killer,' Mayne shouted angrily. 'Get after him.'

'You don't fool me with that one. I know a hold-up when I see one. I'll shoot if either of you moves.'

'You jackass,' Kelly accused. 'You're letting a murderer get away.'

'He'll be back here shortly with the sheriff

and meanwhile you can keep your smart mouth shut. While we're waiting you can unbuckle those gunbelts.'

'What's going on here?' Three pairs of eyes turned to see a big man wearing a sheriff's star standing in the doorway.

'Didn't Hannan tell you?' Glynn said. 'These men were trying to rob him.'

Cahill's large, bushy eyebrows moved closer together in a frown. 'Hannan never came near me. I came down here to arrest that murdering little rat. Unless my deputy misinformed me, Marshal, you have just assisted a dangerous criminal to escape. Now stop annoying these men and get to hell out of Bondsville.'

For a second or two Glynn stood there working his mouth in the manner of a freshly landed trout, but finally words came out. 'He can't be. Hannan is a respectable businessman.'

Before any more of the argument was heard, the clatter of a galloping horse came from the street. All looked through the window in time to see Hannan flash past riding hard.

'There goes your respectable business-man,' Cahill told Glynn contemptuously.

The hero of the Wolf Mountains Battle suddenly looked very sheepish. 'He looked like he was being held up,' he said.

'But neither of us had drawn a gun,' Kelly reminded him, as he rubbed his aching head.

'I'd be happy to postpone my departure and join a posse to go after Hannan,' Glynn said eagerly.

'Don't postpone anything: just get out of town,' Cahill growled.

'I'd be happy to join your posse, Sheriff,' Mayne said. 'Maybe Joe would too, depending upon how his head feels.'

'It feels like I've had it split open with an axe, but I'll live. If you need another volunteer I'll be keen to go with you.'

'Suits me, let's get our horses,' the sheriff said.

'Are you sure you don't need an experi-

enced law-enforcement officer with you?'
Glynn knew how the word would spread
around town and was seeking to redeem his
now severely dented reputation.

'Damn sure. Just make certain you're on
the stage that's leaving today, and the next
time you're talking to President Johnson,
tell him not to bother sending you in this
direction again.'

TWENTY

Hannan was not a particularly good horse-
man and rode hard with the sole intention
of getting away from town as quickly as
possible. He knew he would be followed, so,
after studying the ground, he turned off the
road on a hard patch of earth that did not
show hoofprints very well. Tracking would
be harder as he wove his way around clumps
of mesquite and cactus and rode through

long stretches where sagebrush would partially conceal his tracks.

Sheriff Cahill was an hour behind his man. He had deputized Kelly and Mayne as well as two others and the five rode at a fairly leisurely pace. Cahill saw no point in ruining good horses when the fugitive himself presented so little challenge. Hannan was not considered a violent man and, as a townsman nearly all his life, it was doubtful as to how well he would survive on the open prairie.

Cahill saw no real problem. 'He won't get far. Cedric Hannan couldn't ride in a boxcar unless the doors were sealed and his shirt-tail nailed to the floor. He can twist and turn in all directions but he has to eat and to do that I reckon he'll head for Dallas.'

Kelly was not so sure. 'What's to stop him going north?'

'The fear of Comanches. War parties are still out north of here. The army's chasing them but they're not having a lot of success.'

'Does Hannan know about the Comanches?' Mayne asked.

'He would for sure,' Cahill told him. 'It was the talk of the town and folks around Bondsville were getting mighty jumpy. Hannan was never one to take risks and had a real fear of Indians. He made no secret of it. We're heading for Dallas and will gain a lot of ground on Mr. Hannan while he's riding about trying to bamboozle us.'

Kelly disagreed. 'I'm not sure he's as dumb as that. If he heads north toward the Brazos or the Red, he'll meet up with buffalo-shooting outfits and could get helped by them.'

'There's also Comanches, Kiowas and Southern Cheyenne around the buffalo,' Mayne argued. 'He could meet them just as likely as he could meet white men. I think he'll head for Dallas.'

Kelly was unsure, so they compromised. He and Mayne would take a more northerly approach and the other three would follow the road. Communication might present a few difficulties but all expected that signal shots would bring them together when they found Hannan's tracks.

Machin, or Marlowe as he now called himself, finally found the small bunch of cattle he had been seeking since early morning. He had been in the saddle since the time the trail herd had stampeded. While others held most of the re-gathered cattle on a good patch of grass, a few riders had been sent to find the bunches of steers that had split off during the rush and were scattered away from the main herd. The cattle had taken a long time to settle down at night and the previous night had been only one of several occasions that they had stampeded. Taking wild steers up the trail from Texas was not a job for a man who liked his sleep.

Far to the east, Marlowe saw the dust rising as other riders brought in bunches of lost cattle. They would rest for the remainder of the day and tomorrow would count the herd and start moving north again.

He was tired and not as alert as usual as he directed his charges around a high clump of rocks. The cattle scattered again as they rounded the boulders and the man, by reflex action, started after them without seeing what had spooked them. A sledge-hammer blow in the back of the left shoulder, the report of a gun and the ground seemingly springing up to meet him, left him in no doubt that he had been shot.

He hit his head as he landed and did not see the small man hurrying toward him with a smoking revolver in his hand.

Hannan's one thought was to secure his victim's horse. He had fallen from his own and it had trotted away. Previously he had knotted the reins together so reduce the risk of losing one and they had remained on the horses neck, allowing it to escape unhampered.

One of the fallen man's big .44s had fallen from its holster and Hannan snatched it up. He was aware of the limitations of his .31 pocket revolver. Then he heard galloping horses.

Kelly and Mayne heard the shot that

brought down Marlowe and in the distance saw a riderless horse emerge from behind some rocks.

'There's trouble ahead. Be careful,' Kelly called, as he jumped his mount into a gallop.

Hannan peered from behind a mesquite bush and recognized the two riders. Kelly was a couple of lengths ahead. He would be the first target, but only when he was so close that a hit was almost certain. By the time Mayne saw Kelly knocked from his saddle, he, too, would be an easy target.

The revolver sights were lined on the rider's faded grey shirt when Hannan heard behind him, the ominous double click of a revolver being cocked. A hasty glance over his shoulder saw Marlowe on the ground, bloodstained and dusty, but aiming a revolver directly at him. He knew then that he had turned too late.

Marlowe squeezed the trigger and the big gun sent it's .44 bullet straight into Hannan's chest. The stricken man was slammed back into a nearby boulder before falling sideways to the ground. Involuntarily his finger jerked the trigger of his cocked weapon as he fell and sent a shot skywards.

Kelly reined in his horse as he saw the scene he had ridden into. Powdersmoke hung in the air and two men, still clutching guns, lay on the ground. He recognized both.

'Machin, what happened?'

'The name's Marlowe now. That sonofabitch over there bushwhacked me and was trying to do the same to you. Who was he?'

'His name's Hannan. Among other things, he arranged the killing of Travis Neal and was behind a lot of murders and crooked land deals.'

Though it hurt him, Marlowe laughed. 'Well, don't that beat all. The gun I killed him with was one of Neal's guns that you gave to me. There is some justice in the world after all.'

'How badly are you hit?' Mayne asked.

'I'm not sure. Probably my shoulder's busted. If that's a Colt .31 I see lying near the dear departed I might get out of it lightly. They don't have a lot of power behind them. But I reckon I'll be out of action for a while. I'd be obliged if one of you could catch my horse and take me back to the herd. You can see the dust over there.'

'What if we try to bring the chuck wagon over for you?' Mayne suggested.

'Hell, no. I'm shot, but I ain't dead, and there's some loose steers need chasing up again.'

'You're really taking this droving work seriously,' Kelly said.

'Damn right I am. Me and the others have the start of a respectable life under new names and we're not going to mess it up.'

Mayne chuckled. 'No doubt President Johnson is sleeping easier knowing that Henry Glynn has saved the county from disaster.'

'They're coming,' Anna called, as she stood beside the wagon and watched the two riders splashing across the ford. Her mother and two brothers ceased their work and joined her.

'They're still together,' Norton said. 'I'm not sure if that's a good or a bad sign.'

Mayne dismounted, dropped his reins and threw his arms around his wife and daughter. His two sons crowded around but their joy at seeing him safe was also tempered by a degree of anxiety.

The smile faded from Ethel's face. 'Do we still have a ranch, Dan?'

'We don't, but I got my money back from Hannan before he met a well-deserved end. Don't look so upset, my girl. I took out a homestead claim adjacent to Joe's ranch and Norton and Ollie are old enough to ride to Bondsville and do the same. We can still make our home here on Buffalo Creek.' He turned to Kelly. 'Tell them about the deal we worked out, Joe.'

'We can form a partnership between us, pooling our work with equal shares. We need a couple of cabins, corrals to hold cattle and a couple of fenced pastures for holding our horses and the cattle we round up for sale. We'll have a lot of backaches and blisters before we are finished but we will all have something to show for our efforts. How does the idea sound to you folks?'

There was no dissent.

Kelly unsaddled his horse and rubbed its back before letting it go. He was watching the animal rolling in the dust when Anna came over and stood beside him.

'I'm glad you're back, Joe,' she said shyly.

Kelly thought he had never seen her looking more beautiful. 'That makes two of us, Anna. I missed being away from you. I know I haven't known you long but it's nice having you around.'

The girl smiled and said softly, 'I could be around for a long time now.'

'I sure hope so,' Kelly said fervently. 'I sure hope so.'

The publishers hope that this book has given you enjoyable reading. Large Print Books are especially designed to be as easy to see and hold as possible. If you wish a complete list of our books please ask at your local library or write directly to:

Dales Large Print Books
Magna House, Long Preston,
Skipton, North Yorkshire.
BD23 4ND

This Large Print Book, for people
who cannot read normal print,
is published under the auspices of
THE ULVERSCROFT FOUNDATION